The Art of Cheating Episodes: S1E3

HoLLy BeLLigerence

EXTENDED AUTHOR'S CUT EDITION

HoLLyRod

COPYRIGHT

The Art of Cheating Episodes is a short-story work of fiction inspired by real events. Certain names, places, dialogue, characterizations, and incidents have been altered for purposes of dramatization and to protect the privacy and livelihood of all referenced or involved.

Road to Closure
TAOC Prelude
Episode III

April 2012

"...sunglasses and Advil...
...last night was mad real...
Sun coming up – 5am...
...I wonder if they got cabssss still...."

    Kanye West bars flow loudly from my speakers. The bass from the subwoofers in the trunk got my Lac shaking with heavy vibrations. And it somehow feels like I'm driving *My Precious* even faster now that the silence in the air has ended. Perhaps that's just the power of the music.

    The music always feels so right during times like this. It's almost as if...as soon as it hits yo earlobes, you suddenly got the strength to face even your biggest fears. Sometimes it don't even matter what song is playing. The drumline, the instruments, the way the voice reverberates so organically against the track – it just creates this type of energy that can be unexplainable at times.

    Where would I be without the music?

    Just thinking about that hypothetical is a real mind fuck. Lately I can't tell if being forced to distance myself from the music has been for better or for worse. Pops always told me it could be a little of both. Whatever that means.

"...thinking 'bout the girl in all-leopard...
...who was rubbing the wooD like Kiki Shepard
Two tattoos, one read: 'No Apologies'
...The other said: 'Love is Cursed By Monogamy'"

These lyrics hitting different right now though; I can see the universe is full of hidden messages tonight. And this song is ironically fitting for the backdrop of tonight's chase. If they made a soundtrack to my life...this would most definitely be on it.

"Man we gotta run that back," I reach for the touchscreen tv display in the dashboard. *"This nigga spitting dawg!"*

"Oh whatever nigga. You just high," the beast continues the hating. *"I thought we was riding in silence? Turn that shit off! We gotta hear ourself think, ain't that what you said?"*

"I'ma just let the music tell it since you still in denial!" I jab back. *"What – you all salty about the 'last night was mad real' line?? Why you hating dawg? I did that."*

"Cuz you tryna be funny n'shit! That story wasn't even that dope. You was still sloppy without me, whenever you get through."

"Shit, I can't tell," I refuse to let my greatness be downplayed. *"Hangover nigga! Not even one small detail about that shit ever got back to Kells. Nothing...not a single trace of evidence."*

"Yeah, until she get her hands on your little confession tapes from

tonight. You still sloppy without me."

"*Maaaan…just gimme my fuckin' props! And what you tell me earlier? KeLLy ain't tripping off us all these years later! She could care less — right?*"

"Yeah, so why are we tripping off Kells again?"

"*The deja vü told us to, nigga. Simple signs for the conscious mind. It's obvious the Curse is talking to us — you just don't want me to listen.*"

"Cuz you still ain't made it make no sense for it to be so 'obvious'. What have we learned so far tonight that helps us get the up on Sug? Nothing. I mean — besides the fact that you need me, like you always have. Good thing I'm still here to save yo ass."

"*Whatever, dawg. I can't even hear you right now. The music too loud.*"

The time reads **3:06am**. The thunder and lightning are heavier now, raindrops splashing aggressively against my windshield. I've taken a detour of sorts, now traveling north on *23 Highway* through Valley City and towards Concordia. I've had to slow down on this smaller, narrow road, but I know once I hit Interstate-70 in a few miles, I'll be able to pick up the pace once again.

Until then, I'm letting the music take my mind away. They say an idle mind can be the devil's playground…and my thoughts have continued to bounce from wall to wall in the still, quiet air. So now I'm thinking maybe it wasn't such a good idea to ride in silence, after all. Besides, the music plays an integral part in how I got here tonight.

Maybe it's time I get lost in it all over again.

"...Human beings in a mob...
...what's a mob to a king???
What's a king to a gawd??
...What's a gawd to a non-believeeeeeerrrrr who
don't believe innnn anythinnnnggg???"

Frank Ocean's harmony sums my adrenaline-filled journey up so beautifully:

"...Will he make it out alive? Alright, alrightttt...
...No church in the willld..."

Music is in my bloodline. As much as I initially tried to stray away from my family roots and the powerful influence destiny tends to carry, the fate of my existence forever rests in the energy behind the music.

Lemme explain.

I was the firstborn son of the legendary disc jockey known as *Rockin' Reverend Rod* – the famous soulful radio personality from Lincoln University fame. In the late 70s & early 80s, my Pops was all over the airwaves in the capitol of Missouri, first in his singing group *Black Soul* as *Hollywood Rod*, and then as the *'Righteous Rockin Reverend Rod'* on his late-night radio show called *The Slow Groove*.

The first bedtime stories I can remember were all about Pops' days in the industry. Although his fame would only achieve regional notoriety, and he made a hasty decision to leave the spotlight shortly after I was born, my dad always felt that he had gotten his foot far enough in to keep the door open. Subsequently, and perhaps against my mother's wishes, Pops managed to keep me around all of the music industry madness as a young toddler. He continued to DJ concerts after graduation and kept hundreds of records in the basement of our new Kansas City home.

I had the honor of learning about and becoming familiar with all the musical legends through Pops and his stories…hell I could emulate just about all the famous *Motown* artists by the time I was 6. And before I was old enough to refuse, my dad always had me in somebody's talent show, trying to develop me into a performer. He even hired a dance coach to give me personal training lessons. Pops was determined for me to take over his legacy, in spite of the fact that I never inherited his soulful singing voice.

My parents' separation & divorce put a stop to all'at, and life changed when Mama – suddenly and mysteriously eager to get as far away from Pops & the music as she could – moved me & my younger sister, Ronnie out to Cali for a new start. My folks never explained to us why they were breaking up, but one thing was clear – Mama was not a fan of Pops' music aspirations.

However, relocating to California was only short-lived after we were forced to move *back* home to *Missouri* about a year later – this time to *Saint Louis*, after Mama fell down hard on her luck as a single mother with 2 kids. Things just all seemed to move in a different direction of instability after that, steering me away from the stage…and driving my sister Ronnie down a completely darker path altogether. Losing Mama to cancer a just few years later hit harder than a ton of bricks, and the two of us were then sent *back* to Kansas City to live with Pops – separated from our then 1-year old brother, Lil Jonnie, who had a different father.

Pops still had dreams of me getting in the music business, but by my teenage years I had transitioned into a mere *fan* of music, with a huge amount of respect and appreciation for the art form behind it. After all that time away from Pops, it just wuttin' in my heart to become an artist once puberty hit. My passion rested in writing and I leaned more heavily on the poetry. Pops would tell me back then how connected our destinies were, but when it came to the *music*…I had little inspiration to be involved other than as a listener.

Pops wasn't modest about his disappointment. It was almost as if he needed me to live out his dreams in the music world…he was always talking about legacy and destiny. It was during these adolescent years when Pops first had those talks with me about the **Son's Curse**. The first conversation, however, is the one I always replay in my head…like I'm doing again tonight.

January 1994

One day, he sits me down and tells me it's time to have a serious talk. He opens up with how ironic it is that most of his life, he was told *not* to pursue music…while it's been the opposite for his firstborn son, with how he's stayed in my ear about the industry. He asks my thoughts on it, but at 14 years old, I didn't know how I was supposed to react to that revelation. I didn't understand why that even mattered.

It hadn't been quite a year since Mama had passed away, and I was still getting used to being in a new city as a high school freshman. The adjustment hadn't been easy, and I still had so many questions – about life in general. The relationship between Pops and I had been rocky, but I had developed a sense of comfort in the fact that I was growing up with a father again. So even though I didn't always comprehend the angle of our new interactions, I made it a point to just appreciate these random talks for the principle.

Pops then tells me that part of being a man is realizing that life will continue to teach, and you have to be willing to keep learning regardless of how old you get. He says that he recently learned some deep information about the man who birthed him, my grandfather, and he needs to bring me up to speed about the destiny of our bloodline.

See, Pops never had a relationship with his own father. He says that his dad had a whole other family – a wife and kids – in the state of Illinois. In other words, my dad's mother, known to me as Grandma Dottie, was a side chick who knew my grandad was no good.

Grandpapa Jerry was a known rolling stone. Born and raised in the Chicago area, he had exceptional natural talent for playing the drums. Following the trend of young black kids nationwide at the time, by the age of 16 he dropped out of high school to pursue music fulltime. The same year, he married his pregnant high school girlfriend.

In the late 1930's, Grandpa Jerry was part of a band of jazz musicians who travelled all over the country, oftentimes performing in the legendary Vine District of Kansas City, Missouri. Kansas City had become the perfect playground for the thriving jazz movement. Corrupt politicians allowed for the mob's organized crime to prosper, thus creating an open world for the illegal nightlife to exist. Speakeasys and nightclubs in Kansas City ignored all the liquor and hours-of-operation laws, fostering a culture of drug-induced jam sessions lasting 'til well past sunrise. This non-stop nightlife would give birth to a new 'Kansas City style' of jazz, where musicians would engage in all-night battles of extended soloing, more elaborate riffing, and arranging in the head rather than sight-reading written music.

Grandpa Jerry made a name for himself in Kansas City during this time as *'Drummer Boy Jerry'*. Performing in the same venues as KC legends such as *Count Basie*, *Big Joe Turner*, and an up-and-coming *Charlie 'Bird' Parker*, my grandpapa became fully immersed in the entertainer lifestyle…and all of the temptations that came along with it. The women became as big a drug for Drummer Boy Jerry as the heroin he notoriously couldn't get enough of.

They say he liked to boast about finding a dame to have his child in every different city he performed in regularly. They say that the first night Grandpa Jerry met my Grandma Dottie in the Vine District, he told her she would be his 'KC mama' one day. Still married to her first husband at the time, Grandma Dottie simply shrugged him off and pretended she wasn't flattered. For years, however, they say Drummer Boy Jerry would publicly flirt and fancy Grandma Dottie whenever he was in town.

Pops says 'they' never really say *how* it happened, but I start to immediately wonder if Grandma Dottie left her first husband...chasing a dream of flashing lights with Grandpa Jerry. I wonder if he ever gave her reason to believe that he would someday leave his family back home in Chicago. Surely, she had to know about his reputation that preceded him...right? *Something* had to compel my Grandma Dottie to get caught up in Grandpa Jerry's mystique...something *powerful* had to draw her in against otherwise better judgement. I mean – she had two kids by the son of a bitch.

Pops tells me he only saw his father twice in his lifetime. Once when Grandpa Jerry came to pick him and his younger sister, my Aunt Bev, up for ice cream...and again the following year at Grandpa Jerry's funeral when Pops was 14.

It was on that ice cream date that Grandpa Jerry talked to my young father about his remorse for not being there for him and Aunt Bev. Grandpa claimed that he had lived a reckless life because of mishandling the **Son's Curse**, and he feared that this curse would be handed down to all his male offspring. Pops says it's all Grandpa Jerry talked about until he dropped them back off with Grandma Dottie that day.

Pops told me that because he had grown up without a father and it felt good to finally bond with the man he'd never known – that **Son's Curse** nonsense stuck with him.

But he also thought my grandpa was just a crazy, deadbeat junkie...so at first, Pops didn't take any of it too seriously. The older Pops got, however, the more he started to see some of the things Grandpa Jerry warned him about before his untimely death. Sounds familiar...I know.

'No matter what you do to them, women will love you blindly and you won't be able to get rid of certain ones forever,' Pops tells me days before my 15th birthday. *'The Son's Curse, my boy. I know it sounds crazy, but just hear me out. I'm not gonna be around forever, son, so you've gotta figure out a way to not bite off more than you can chew.'*

It was confusing to hear my dad tell me to take heed to the advice of a dead man who never stepped up to the plate. Pops resented this muthafucka, even at a young age I picked up on how hard he strived to be nothing like Grandpa Jerry. So why should I respect any fake wisdom the deadbeat tried to hand down to us?

Pops tells me that I'm at that age where I can't escape fate. He tells me that it's important that I take all of this seriously, telling me how he doesn't want me to follow in his and Grandpa Jerry's footsteps. This is where he lost me. My dad was nothing like Grandpa Jerry. He was always telling me how sick he was during the years he was separated from me and Ronnie, because of a personal vow he made to be in his kids' life no matter what. I knew that having a deadbeat daddy had taken its toll on my Pops and he was dedicated to becoming the man his father never was. So, I was confused at the way he compared himself to Grandpa Jerry and demanded an explanation.

'I hear you son. But sometimes we pick up traits from those who came before us. We are who we are. Your Grandma Dottie used to tell me I was just like your grandpa – no matter how much I hated her saying it. I'm realizing now that I'm more like Mr. Jerry than I ever wanted to believe. We walked the same paths, son."

'With what – the music? Ok…so what you wanted to be just like your daddy and get into music? Lots of boys wanna do what dey daddy did – if Moms ain't keep us from you during the split, I prolly woulda did the same thing! So what??'

'That's the thing I'm tryna tell you Rod. Remember what I just said? I saw my daddy twice in life. The only conversation I ever had with him was about this Son's Curse. I had no idea who he was in the music world.'

'So wait,' I paused, trying to absorb the thought. *'You saying that…'*

'…that I got into music coincidently, without ever even knowing the history of Drummer Boy Jerry's legacy, son.'

Pops continued, explaining how my aunt Beverly found a newspaper clipping of Grandpa Jerry while home for the holidays the previous month and that prompted the two siblings to do some digging. He says that Grandma Dottie always hid who Grandpa Jerry was from them, reminding me how none of us had Mr. Jerry's last name. Still, I was blown away at the fact that Pops had no idea his dad was a jazz legend, yet he still ironically chose the same path of music as his predecessor. What were the odds?

Pops then gets deep on me. He starts talking about the energy of the Curse and how he now understands that that's what drew him to music. He says there's no other way to explain how he was never exposed to his father's roots and yet the music still found its way to his path.

*'So you saying...the curse...is **the music?**'* I was still struggling to understand.

'No. Think of it this way. You're like a irresistible magnet – for feminine energy. Women will be drawn to you, even when you give them reason not to be. That's the Son's Curse. The entrapment of energy that won't go away if left unsettled. That's the simplest way I can put it.'

'But like...energy from what? The power of music??? You making my head hurt Pops.'

Pops eases my anxiety by saying that he's pushing 40 years old and still learning about how the Curse works to this day. He explains that the Curse *is not* the music, and that the women are drawn in from the gift of gab and the ability to express ourselves more uniquely than most. This confuses me even more since I still can't see what the Curse has to do with the music.

He then tells me the music aspect is a ***second*** tier to our man-to-man conversation. He starts talking about the power of music, and how living with something like the Son's Curse can be even worse when coupled with the talent of musical creativity. He reiterates how things have started to make more sense to him now that he's aware of his father's history. He talks about his own experience in the music industry and how the level of temptation was far worse during his days as an artist. He asks me if I knew that his affiliation with music played a role in my Moms asking for a divorce.

Of course I knew that. It's lowkey one of the reasons I strayed away from the idea of continuing Pops' legacy – feeling like the music contributed to breaking up my family. I kind of see where he going, but I ain't feeling it. Pops was having some guilt about the way his dad abused the music, yet I wuttin' seeing the comparison. Cuz the way my dad chased the music was totally different – Pops ain't go around knocking up girls state-to-state like they say Grandpa Jerry did.

But Pops says that it's the way the Curse works, how it carries energy. He says that if you learn how to pay attention to the signs, you can hear what it's trying to tell you. My Grandma Dottie hated Pops' interest in music…something my old man could never understand before he had knowledge of Grandpa Jerry's career. He tells me how he had to hide his pursuit from Grandma until he was far away at college. Then, he says, months before my mama became pregnant with me…she, too, started pressuring him to let the music go. All of a sudden, he says.

This naturally prompted me to ask Pops what he was out here doing to make *Mama* hate the music the same way Grandma Dottie did. My grandma had good reason, with how Grandpa Jerry had been reckless. But to my knowledge, *Pops* hadn't inherited the same habits. Right?

He tiptoes around it, saying the point of all of this isn't to trip off what *his* past actions may have been. The point is, now that Pops has learned about his dad's past, today he can go back and interpret what the Curse was truly trying to tell him over the years.

'Now I feel like that was the Curse fussing at me through your mama and grandma. Your mama would say the same things your grandma said – it almost felt like a **deja vü**. The Curse will talk to you through **deja vüs** like that through the universe, to warn you when you doing too much. When you headed down a risky path, you gon feel a **deja vü**. You gotta learn how to find a way to listen.'

"So that was the Curse telling you not to do music because of Grandpa Jerry's mistakes? Ok, so then good. Then I won't do music, and I won't have a bunch of baby mamas all over the place. And then I won't have to worry about the Curse. Problem solved."

'Slow down, son. It's not that simple. You'll never get rid of the Curse, it's in your bloodline. What I want you to take away from this is to just start being mindful. Learn how to pay attention to the signs and make better decisions with the energy you'll attract. If not, the decisions can reappear, and it'll feel like history is repeating itself. What I'm trying to figure out right now...is how your Grandpa Jerry's music path carried over into **my** journey. Somehow his energy with the music found its way into my world, without influence.'

'But...does that mean the Curse is **karma***?'*

'I don't know if I'd say it's **karma** son. I think the energy and soul ties being mishandled can **lead** to karma, though. Unsettled emotions, consequences of decisions. Something in the way Grandpa Jerry handled the energy that came along with the music carried it over to me. Maybe it was how he chased that fantasy of having kids outside his marriage. I ain't figured out what it means yet, but it means **something**. Something was left without closure...and it came back around for me to make a better decision. That same decision has always been in front of you, son.'

'So then I should just stay away from the music then, right?'

'That's the thing, son. For me, I kept seeing and hearing messages to leave it alone. But with **you**, it's been the opposite. All you heard your whole life was that you was supposed to pick up where I left off.'

'Man, I don't get it Pops! All of this is just dumb!' I threw my hands up in frustration.

'Son,' Pops chuckled. '*I don't expect you to get it overnight – I'm still tryna figure out what it all means. I just expect you to remember what I told you today. Pay attention, son. There's a cycle with the music that the Curse wants us to alter. That could mean two different things for us, Rod. You gotta find out what it means for you.'*

'Whatever man. I ain't thinking 'bout being no rapper, and I can't even sing. The Curse ain't gotta worry about lil ole me with the music, Pops. I'm straight, dude.'

*'Ok, Rod. All I know is this: Whatever you decide with that, son, will be one of the biggest decisions you ever make. The decision **will** show up for you Rod, maybe multiple times before it's all said and done. Just remember I said that. Do not ignore the signs.'*

April 2012

The rain is really pouring down as I approach the ramp to get on Interstate-70 East. It's now **3:14am**. If my intel was correct, that puts me about forty-five minutes behind Sug's distance ahead of me to St. Louis. I'm still making good timing.

I eventually learned how to pay attention to the messages in the universe Pops told me about that day. But I made it all through college and to my mid-twenties before I jumped into music. By then, the Curse had shown me far too many signs that I was indeed destined to pursue music and it seemed to make sense.

There's truth to my inner beast's claim that I needed him. For the music…I did. I needed the energy of the beast to find my voice on the mic…to find confidence in my presence. Before *KeLLy's Revenge*, and prior to the uncaging of my beast…I wouldn't have given music a second thought. I ignored the signs routinely, afraid to become another Grandpa Jerry. Once the beast was in the picture, however, those same signs spoke a different message to me. I started to ask, 'what if the Curse intended for *me* to handle the music in ways that Drummer Boy Jerry couldn't???' Pops always said he and I might be getting different messages…right? After *KeLLy's Revenge*, it felt like maybe I was supposed to alter our bloodline's cycle by running *towards* the music instead of away from it. The beast made it easier for me to take that dive.

But the deeper I got off into my craft, the further apart Kells and I grew. The temptations and opportunities were bigger, like Pops said they would be. The groupies came almost overnight. Then I met *Sashé*, the internet model sensation who would become my new play toy on the side. Before I was done recording my first project, Kells and I broke up for good…and I ended up with Sashé. Thinking back on it all over again now…it's almost as if when I left KeLLy for Sashé, I left Kells for *the music.*

The Curse deja vü'd the *Warrensburg* sign tonight – to point to *KeLLy's Revenge*. And before *KeLLy's Revenge* there was no real belligerence…there was no beast uncaged. Chasing new fantasies fueled and empowered my inner beast…but before all of that…there was no music. In the end, music still became that same gateway to new levels of boldness, like with my Grandpapa Jerry and Pops before me.

Where would I be without the music? Definitely less belligerent, HoLLy…

*   *   *   *   *

…to be continued in TAOC Episodes S1E3

*Have you ever seen a picture or a portrait —
full of beautiful color and intricate detail, so
complex and deep, and exploding with pure
artistry???? Give it but a glance and you'll never
appreciate the true brilliance behind it.
Yet...stare at it for too long....and you'll
become consumed by its mystique and engrossed
to near obsession.*

Cheating is a work of art.

This...

*...is the masterpiece that I've always liked to
call...*

The Art of Cheating

1

*Ok so listen up, this is a story about the **belligerence of my inner beast** and struggling to live with dangerous decisions. It's not for the weak or fragile heart.*

****YOU'VE BEEN WARNED ****

The episode starts off *circa 2009*…so we're jumping around again. But here's why:

I consider this a major pivotal point in my *Art of Cheating* episodes. I was at a crossroads. Fully involved with the music. A long, storied, and successful career of being the ultimate *playboy*. And now I'm once again in a position to either learn from my mistakes or become further consumed by them. This is where the string of events that sent me on the ***road to closure*** first started.

There's a lot of shit I can't unpack all at once yet, so I'm only gonna focus on the key pieces this episode. Stay with me.

It's the end of the summer. I am now technically a single man – and I say *technically* for a reason. So let's catch up.

KeLLy and I have been broken up for about 4 years now. I won't tell the story yet of *how* we broke up…the whole breakup story isn't needed here. It is necessary to explain some things about the separation, however, because what happened *after* that helped create the *monster* inside the beast of today's storyline.

Ok. So, I left KeLLy (*yes, again…I left **her***) for a younger, bubbly, bisexual chick who introduced me to a whole new world of xxxcitement. Let's call her what we've been calling her – *Shay* – short for *Sashé*.

Shay and I had a very open relationship. Not open as in '*open lines of communication and honesty*' – though we did have that element for the most part. But open as in…we were borderline swingers. She loved chicks as much as I did and was cool with me fucking other women. We had plenty of ***ménages***, orgies, and wild nights together…as a happy couple.

My relationship with Shay was unique in the fact that for the time I was with her…I cheated the *least*. My family had been thrown into the spotlight with Ronnie's highly publicized murder case, which meant we were also thrown into the line of fire with the ongoing turf war in the city. I cheated the least with Sashé partly because I had to switch up the way I was moving in these KC streets with bitches. But I also no longer had reason to sneak around to keep my beast fed. With Shay, from the very beginning, I could talk about my urges with others *as well as* act out on them. It took me a while to adjust to that, but the closer we got,

2

the more I gave in to the concept of being completely faithful. Shay *loved* to watch me fuck another chick in front of her. That new lifestyle catered to my greedy habits and it felt like the perfect fit. This was the scope of my everyday life for the years prior to today's story.

So Shay and I did our thing up until 2008, about a year before where this story begins. That year, we went through this *huge* breakup that left me *HURT* as fuck. I mean *hurt*. Like *WHO HURT YOU* type hurt.

I came home from work one day in the summer to find all of her shit moved out, she'd suddenly had enough. Now remember, I cheated the *least* with Shay, so when we broke up – I had no other chicks on the side. So to come home and find that she's moved out and left me with all the bills four months before the lease was up – that shit *killed* me. I remember feeling like not knowing how to move on. I just couldn't swallow the fact that after the playboy life I led before…I could now actually be *alone*. I went from waking up daily with multiple chicks all in the same bed…to waking up on an air mattress watching porn.

And then the reason *why* Shay left is even more crazy. Again, I won't go into full detail here. It's hard to make a long story short, but it was devastating to say the least. In a nutshell, after we had our sexcapades and mutually let each other explore desires with no limits…she ended up leaving me to start fucking with *chicks only*.

OUCH.

3

SERVES me RIGHT.

iKnow.

Karma is clever...

For weeks after Shay left, I was a sick puppy. Sashé and I had a nearly perfect partnership with no drama. Seemed so made for and in tune with each other. And then all of a sudden, once we had that first fight after almost *three years* – shit just went sour really quick. I was a crushed man.

But *karma's clever*...I suppose. As time went on, I started to feel that maybe it was meant for me and Shay to implode like that. I mean, it was bound to happen – right? Ultimately, I'd made the bed I was left lying in, with how I'd broke up with KeLLy for one of my side chicks. And so, because of that, I wanted to believe that Sashé walking out on me was my rightful payback and lesson to be learned for the way I left *Kells* for her. I wanted to accept that my irreparable mistake had been letting myself get so close to Shay in the first place, given the fact that she started as a side bitch. That was a cardinal sin in the *Art*, and it served me right.

Right???

Still, I was emotionally destroyed when Shay left...and my inner beast just wouldn't allow me to fully blame myself. I'll never forget that piercing surge stinging in my chest on the day I came home to that empty apartment.

4

June 2008

"Fuck that. You know we don't believe in karma in HoLLyWorld, nigga," that familiar, sinister voice reminded me.

"Man but her energy feels so strong with this shit bro. It's gotta be her. This time, it has to be," I was thoroughly convinced.

"Dawg, that's bullshit! Fuck Karma! We was all in with Shay! You know that... and she knows that! She owed you more than this, HoLLy."

"Yeah, but still. This is still on me. Right? I shoulda knew this day was coming. Deep down, it feel like I was supposed to expect shit to end like this with Shay. You know we wasn't supposed to last this long, dawg. Look at how we started."

"Don't you even bring up KeLLy, nigga," the beast interjects sharply, already knowing where my thoughts are going.

"It was a cardinal sin in the **Art,** *bro. We knew that. Nigga... and I know you feel this shit stinging,"* I placed my hand on my chest, trying to ease the pain. *"It's that same type of fucking hurt. That night on the highway."*

"Nah... this is different," he insists I'm overanalyzing again. He despises when I overthink shit like this.

"I know this heartache too well, bro. Like way too well. It feels even worse this time."

5

"And that's why it's not a deja vù. This ain't the Curse talking to you this time. The pain is different, like you just said, HoLLy."

"It's close enough, though! This shit hurts, bro...it really fucking hurts! At the very least...this gotta be related to how we left Kells! How do you not see that??? Come on, dawg, it's deja vù."

"Yeah, but it feel worse this time. It feel worse because you know we ain't deserve this. Not this. Not from Shay. We gave her everything, HoLLy. No Lies. We gave her everything."

"No lies," I repeat in cadence from habit. *"That's real talk. I gave Shay all of me. I gave that girl everything."*

"Everything...but a reason. Remember, you said KeLLy's Revenge was Kells' payback for yo sloppiness. Kells had a reason, you said it yourself."

"Yeah, but still. I hurt Kells after all'at. When I left."

"Fuck that karma shit, bro. This wuttin' KeLLy who just left us for dead, nigga — this was Shay! And Shay never had a reason for this!"

"Fuck bro!! You ain't have to do this shit, Shay!!!" it hurts deeply to admit it to myself. But it's true. Shay never had a reason.

"Dawg, not like this. She gotta pay for crossing us, HoLLy."

That first time my inner ~~beast~~ threw it out there, I shrugged it off and pretended it wasn't my own voice talking that nonsense. To plot against the woman I was in love with was an unthinkable thought. But what was even

6

more difficult to process...was the thought of Sashé, the woman who I had also went against my principles for, being seduced into becoming a tool of punishment for my own past behavior. That cut deep, making it a challenge to truly believe I deserved it.

How could I *not* have real resentment towards Sashé?? She shoulda been stronger, and not let anything come between us. *Right?* She had switched up on me, and *her* new habits, not mine, caused us to grow apart. Again – my cheating had *stopped* with Sashé, I was all in before she left. Punishment for the cardinal sin of leaving KeLLy or not, Shay still owed us so much more than *that*.

Everybody knows the best temporary fix to a broken heart is a bunch of new pussy. But like I said, since my cheating had ceased, I literally had no one else to immediately fall back on. No side chicks, and no potentials. I recovered in solitude. So many sleepless nights; so much lack of appetite. Shay knew I had Ronnie's court case coming up and how major it was. Still, she bailed on me and our luxury apartment as if it were nothing.

Forced to move out, rebuild, and regroup, I was jaded. Sessions with my therapist had been no help. The new pussy I eventually started getting again couldn't take my mind off my heartbreak. I found myself continuing to have the darkest thoughts about my ex.

Then one night, it happened. One night, I decided to finally give in to my inner beast's sinister influence. One night...I asked the *cheat gawds* for a second chance with

Shay.

I literally *asked* the **Son's Curse** to send Shay back
my way – to give me the opportunity to cause her the
same restless nights. With vengeful and angry tears, I
begged for a chance to make Sashé feel the gut-wrenching
pain she'd left me with.

That's where the *Silent Promise* to my ex was born.
Pops said the Curse returns unsettled energy with
purpose, but what happens when it's me who's left
without closure? I needed my fuckin' lick back. So, I made
a vow that if Shay ever crossed my path again, I would
have my revenge. And I promised myself that until that
day came when I could shatter her soul, I'd take it out on
every other bitch along the way in the meantime. I allowed
my beast full freedom at that point, locking my conscience
and morals away in the same cage that used to restrain my
monster.

"It's for the best, HoLLy," it whispered. *"If we spare no one,
this never happens again. All these hoes gotta pay..."*

By summer '09 – I've regained my mojo. Being sick
over Shay becomes a thing of the past and now I'm out
for blood. Suddenly I don't feel like *Grandpa Jerry* was a
villain after all in his day; suddenly his belligerence makes
more sense. His energy fuels a musical spark that makes
me connect more with his story. I start to relate more with
my dark side, feeling like I shoulda never stopped cheating
in the first place. Most of these bitches ain't shit...I can
see that clearly now.

One of the lines in a song I wrote that summer said, *'Twisted is the mind of a nigga scorned.'* That lyric best sums up where I was in the head now, being *'technically single'* and all.

There's that word again.

TECHNICALLY.

I'm technically single, because I don't answer to anybody. But I was *literally* single for maybe only a couple of weeks after Shay left.

'Single' is misused pretty broadly around the world and most people don't mean it literally.

In **HoLLyWorld**, however, we like to establish differences between *technical* vs *literal* meanings. Literally speaking, and by definition, single means *'one or without another'*. Single doesn't mean *non-committed* – which is what most people mean when considering themselves single. But a nigga can be non-committed and also *'not single'*, which is what I mean when I say *technically single*. That's the proper way to describe what *most* people mean when they say they 'single'. They really just be non-committed – which is technically single.

You only *literally* single if it ain't nan another muhfucka in the picture that you can call...for whatever purpose. In my case, I had new bitches on pussy-dial by that summer. But since I wasn't *committed* to any of them, that made me technically single.

9

Now, to get even more technical, there's levels to everything – including being single. I was *emotionally* and *financially* single when Shay left…but *physically-speaking*, I had plenty of access on my newly formed roster. I'm technically single…not literally. The ~~beast~~ helped me build a huge wall to keep bitches out emotionally and financially. Trust me when I say this – this is where the *real* belligerence began.

With KeLLy, I still had a heart – believe it or not – so there were feelings that I went to great lengths to spare. And then with *Shay*…like I've said for the 100th time, I *cheated* the *least*. So even with all the wild shit going on with Sashé, I still kept it honest, fair, and mostly respectable.

In *Summer '09* tho, no feelings were to be spared or considered anymore. I literally had stopped giving a fuck, my rage ignited like never before. I learned to live for the belligerence of my ~~beast~~ and dogging muhfuckaz out. The ~~beast~~ was right, too – cuz it quickly helped me regain and keep my strength going forward.

From a Jedi to a Sith Lord in the mastery of *The Art of Cheating…this* is where we find HoLLy as this story begins.

~~Beast~~ in full control. Out for blood, out for revenge.

July 2009

I'm out clubbing as usual with my folks one night,

doing my thing. **HoLLyShades** and in full character…ya dig? Well, this particular night, I *finally* run into Shay after *eight months* of zero contact. And this muthafucka is looking the best she's ever looked in life on this night. This episode isn't really about her, so I won't describe Shay's features here. Just knowing *who* she is along with our history is enough.

Anyway, I'm caught off guard…bumping into Sashé unexpectedly. I'd eventually started believing we'd never see each other again and maybe I was even hoping we didn't – so I wouldn't have to carry out that unthinkable *Silent Promise*. The very sight of Shay stopped me where I stood. I mean…she's looking a hundred times better than before and she was giving off this energy that I couldn't resist melting from. I missed her, and the more the liquor kept flowing, the more that became a task to hide. At one point, after she ordered yet another round of shots, she leaned in so close I thought she was gonna kiss me. Hell, I almost wanted her to. But then she just mumbled ever so softly how she could tell what I was thinking. She said she was thinking the same thing.

If it wasn't for the ~~beast~~, I might've caved in, and started balling right there at the bar. The usual conflict in my head ensued. I started thinking about all those sleepless nights. I started thinking about how good things were with Shay. I started thinking about how she'd thrown all that away.

"Fuck this bitch, HoLLy. Literally. Let's start keeping her up all night. Tonight."

11

We ended up back at my downtown apartment and fucked all night. Which woulda been right on par for my plot for revenge...except...the sex was amazing. I mean, the sex was always amazing with Sashé. But it seemed like, on *this* night, Shay was on a mission. It had been eight months, and she knew I had been fucking mad bitches. Shay just knew me like that, she knew how I would be coping. But it's like she wanted to prove to me that no matter how much other pussy I'd been getting since our breakup, nobody knew me sexually like she did.

Well after that, we can't stay away from each other, suddenly re-opening the floodgates of emotions and feelings all over again. She wants to patch things up...but I'm still scorned overall. The beast keeps whispering about that *Silent Promise*. But Shay's energy was different than when we fell out and she made it a point to show me just how much.

It was almost working. She kinda still had me...but she ain't '*have* me' have me – y'all know what I mean.

The monster in me was still bitter. Once we linked back up, I realized quickly that I was still soft on her. But at the same time – the opportunity to finally dog Shay out and have the perfect revenge has perfectly presented itself, and I gotta find a way to follow through somehow.

I just need to find the right opportunities to get my lick back with Sashé. It's gonna be harder than I anticipated, but this is what I asked for...right?

12

Ok, so a few more weeks pass, and I'm at this photo shoot for my first album cover. There's a bunch of models...they're half naked...you know how it goes. Ok, well there was this one model in particular that caught my eye immediately...

Let's call her **Lisa**.

Lisa is where this story of *belligerence* begins...

*   *   *   *   *

2

Let's describe *Lisa*. She's about 5'4", and if she's 150 pounds, 30 of that *has* to be her ASS. This chick has one of the fattest asses I've ever laid eyes on.

Y'all know *PINKY,* the porn star? Picture *Pinky.* *Early* Pinky, before the bitch started eating more cheeseburgers than dick – I'm talking about *that* Pinky. That's how much ass Lisa got – the chick is fucking built like a real thoroughbred.

She's cute and young in the face. Big innocent eyes. I mean she prolly not innocent – but compared to *me* – well yeah, I can use the word *innocent.* I'm a fucking beast, so it's safe to say she ain't never met nobody like me before.

And at this point, we haven't officially met at all – I'm just on some creep shit from the back of the room. Watching. Sipping my drink in my plastic cup…paying close attention.

Lisa's standing up front with four other girls, talking to the photographer. She's shorter than the other models, stout thighs and smaller upper body. Her stance is what's killing me at the moment – with her chin up and chest poked out...hands in the small of her back.

"Dude, her ass looks like it's moving while she standing there... "

"I see. Fuck! Man, but she standing still, dawg. I know dat muhfucka ain't moving, bruh."

"Unless it is...nigga."

I mean, I *have* been sipping a little. And then my cousin *Benny* rolled up that kush blunt in the car – that shit got my eyes twitching behind my *HoLLyShades*, so I could be tripping. But then again, this sculpture of an ass *could* very well have a life of its own and truly be animated.

I decide to take a closer look.

They're all standing up front, gathered around the photographer *Trent*, who's sitting at a desk and staring at his laptop. The two taller models are behind Trent, and I can't really recall how the two shorter girls were positioned...but Lisa was standing to the left side of the desk. I'm on the far other side towards the back of the room...but directly across from Lisa and staring at her right cheek.

"I swear it's moving in them stretch pants."

So I start walking towards the front, but sort of diagonal, so it doesn't look like I'm walking right up on Lisa. There's a stereo in front of the desk and the photographer is playing some of my music from the

16

album.

"I'll just act like I'm changing the track," I say to myself.

"Nigga, I don't care how you play it off, just get over there."

Once I reach the middle of the room, Benny hangs up from his phone call and starts walking toward the desk, too. "Aye cuzz, when we getting started?" he asks me impatiently. "Let's go outside for a minute."

I tell him, "Nah, I'm already high, bro."

I'm walking and talking without looking at Benny, eyes locked on *'Lisass'*. We approach the desk. Benny walks to the right, and now I'm in front of the stereo. All of a sudden, Trent and the models are done with their briefing and the girls all start walking off to get dressed for the shoot. Lisa walks by me to my left…making eye contact. At least she tried to…ain't no way she can see my eyes through my *HoLLy's*. But I can see hers just fine…and I stare her down as she walks past, close enough for me to get a whiff of her body spray.

"Damn, this bitch smells lovely," my beast is out for real blood.

I tilt my head completely to my left to watch her walk around me, then I turn quickly to the right as she walks over to the area where Benny was talking on the phone before. There's this privacy wall in place to create a dressing area and she goes behind it to get changed. But there's no actual door to block the view…just a wall in

17

front of the brick corner.

"So, how is this supposed to work? I mean, all I gotta do is walk back to the corner where I was before and I can see clearly behind this wall…"

"Nigga, that's a no-brainer! Head right the fuck back over there, then! Space Age HoLLy shit! Who gon check us?"

*"Right! I don't give a fuck. This **my** photo shoot!"*

The other girls I can't see getting dressed, not that I wanted to. But as fate would have it, Lisa is in plain view once I reach the back wall again. She's kneeling down, slipping her leggings off. She may as well not even wore panties. That thong is nothing more than a string of garment around her waist…you can't even see it other than that.

"Gotdammit, this girl is so fucking thick!!!"

She stands up…pulling a pair of *DymeWear* boy shorts up her thighs, around her full hips, and then finally around her monster booty. She turns to her right, and now she can see me looking.

And I *keep* looking, trying to see her reaction. All I can make out from across the room is a smirk from Lisa, as she continues getting changed…but I *know* she seen me looking. Fuck it – I want her to know I'm looking.

I quickly remind myself that's the most I can do at this moment – just look. Even my cousin and street team

18

manager Benny is keeping it unusually professional, so I gotta keep myself in check. I'm not here for any other purpose than business, and once we snap these flicks for the album cover – I'm out. That was the plan...and I stuck to it.

We posed, Trent snapped, everyone got changed again, and we left. I ain't even pull Lisa to the side or get a hug; I got my creep on in the corner of the room and kept it moving.

A week or so passes...and I can't stop thinking about this Lisa chick. I mean, I'm laid up with Shay...and I'm thinking about that fat juicy ass. I'm laid up with Shay *and* her roommate...yet I can hear the ~~beast~~ whispering, *' ain't neither one of these hoes got a booty like Lisa'.*

I gotta see this ass again – and not just in the pics from my shoot.

I wait 'til early morning, after Sashé and *Kristina*, the roomie, get up outta bed to shower together. They ask me if I'm getting in, I say 'I'm good, I need to send out some emails.'

They head to the bathroom next to Shay's room and I'm in bed on my laptop...logging into *Facebook*.

I do a search for '*Luscious Lisa*'.

19

And now I'm in her *INBOX*…

*   *   *   *   *

3

Lisa wastes no time in responding to my *'Hey you'*
message, just two minutes after it was sent.

The world has come a long way from days where
emailing was the thing. Social media has changed the
game, and this is right before the *Twitter* renaissance. The
lines-of-communication culture is on the brink of
changing forever…and here I am, a nigga from the stone
age turned space age, messaging bitches on this *Facebook*
site. I never missed a beat with this shit.

I'm inboxing Lisa, telling her how dope she was at
the shoot…you know – giving her them mandatory props.
I can tell she's a sweetheart from our exchange, I almost
feel bad for being up to no good. But yo…like I said – it's
a new day and I'm out for blood.

So Shay and Kris start rubbing baby oil on each
other in the mirror in front of me, and I'm laid across the
bed – back to the wall and on my computer – not paying
them much attention. Lisa and I are flirting now…nothing
else matters.

Just like I thought, she knows I watched her undress
at the shoot the other day. She even caught my stare down

as she walked past...she can describe to me how I turned
my head and everything. This is enough to impress me
because if she caught me looking...that means she was
looking too. And since she ain't tripping off me looking at
what I like and liking what I seen...I know that she likes
what she saw as well. And now, *something* has to be done.
So naturally speaking in the cyberworld scope of things –
this is where I ask her:

"So when are we hanging out *offline*?"

Shay suddenly starts complaining about me being on
the internet and so I tell Lisa to gimme her number and
we'll continue this through text later. Thirty seconds
later...I've got the math.

Wait...I'm *technically* single. Right? Why am I getting
off my computer cause of Shay fussing? We aren't
together anymore – *right?* Well, here's the circumstance:

*So, a week or two before my photoshoot, my car gets stolen
from in front of my apartment. I've moved to this small ass
apartment in downtown KCMO alone...trying to continue picking
up from where Shay left me the year before. Well anyway, a nigga car
gets stolen...and recovered about a week later. But my shit is
thrashed...these punk muhfuckaz tore my shit up and I need all
sorts of repairs. With all my finances being tied up in my album
budget, it'll take me about a month to come up with the bread for all
the parts & labor...and I initially refused to accept Shay's offer to
give me the money. I know she cares, but I also know it's part of her
campaign for us to be together again – which I ain't tryna do. This is*

like a deja vü for Sashé and I – she loaned me $$$ for car trouble in the beginning of our relationship, when I was still torn between her and KeLLy. This feels like the Curse bringing a decision back around for me, so I refuse the help.

We end up arguing about this shit. And when I say 'we', I mean me and Shay…and also, me and the **beast***. The* **beast** *feels like this falls right in line with the Silent Promise, but I think that would be taking it too far. So, in the end, I don't take Shay's offer to pay for my repairs…but I agree to use her car for transportation in the meantime whenever necessary. Which means that she gets to see more of me…and on mornings where I needed the car early, I'd have to spend the night at her spot and drop her off at work in the morning. For these weeks – even though me and Shay weren't technically together – she was my main chick again…and all rules of engagement in* **The Art of Cheating** *applied.*

On this Tuesday morning that I'm inboxing Lisa for the first time, I'm over Shay's…counting down the days 'til I get my car up and running again. Planning, plotting on who I'm gonna fuck next…and figuring out how to keep executing my ulterior motives. You know what…it could've been a Thursday tho – I just remember the day of the week being a 'T' day for some reason. The point is – my car would be ready on that Saturday.

Fuck it. Let's just say it's Tuesday…that sounds more accurate.

*   *   *   *   *

It's later that Tuesday night now. I picked up Shay from work around 6pm and dropped her off at home. I'm in traffic again, making a *GG* run before I come back to spend the night with Shay and Kris.

What's *GG*? Oh…of course – in **HoLLyWorld** – *GG* is my pet name for my favorite drug. It's short for green goblin.

So anyway, it's after 7…going on 8. And I'm in Shay's car. On the way back from the goblin man, I text Lisa…on some small talk shit.

ME: "Hey wassup baby girl…"

LISA: "Hey…what's going on…"

Damn that was fast. I still have to get used to how this text shit works…even after years of being on it, it's still amazing how quick you can reach out to a muhfucka these days.

ME: "Shit, out in traffic. How you doing?"

LISA: "Just got out shower. Can u call me?"

ME: "Ok. Gimme a min, driving."

I tell her to gimme a minute cuz I'm driving – but that's just to stall time. I mean it's riskier to text and drive – duh. But I'm really trying to figure out how I'm gonna give her some voice chat when I'm 20 seconds from pulling back up at Shay's.

"Man, just sit outside in the parking lot and talk to the bitch," the ~~beast~~ whispered.

"Damn nigga, I know. Relax. Lemme scope the scene first."

So I pull up in Shay's lot, immediately looking for Kris' car…which is nowhere in sight. She could be at work – I can't remember if she's dancing tonight or not. If she's not at work, and she comes home – me sitting in Shay's parked car, talking on the phone won't be a good look. But I damn sure ain't 'bout to be able to talk to Lisa in the apartment with Shay lounging around…so I decide on the lesser of the two evils, and plan to just keep a lookout for Kris.

It's been about four minutes since I last texted Lisa and she picks up on the 1st ring, "Hello…"

"Aye wassup," I lowered my voice, getting into character.

"Oh nothing," she responded, her volume matching mine. "Just got out the shower…"

"Yeah, that's what you said," I licked my lips. "Mm hmm."

27

"What you say '*mm hmmm*' for???" Lisa wondered.

"No reason," I chuckled. "I just got a visual, that's all."

"Mmm. A visual huh???" Lisa let her mind wander. "See – you bad. I can already tell."

"What you mean??? Bad like *good* or bad like *bad*? What you tryna say, lil mama???" I asked as if I didn't know the answer.

"I mean I'm just saying…maybe a little of both," she admitted with a flirty undertone.

My eyes light up, anticipating where this exchange is heading. Now I can smell the blood in the water.

"Explain," I said with my usual smirk. "I'm a real technical, to-the-point guy, ya dig? I'm into the details."

*   *   *   *   *

4

"Yeah I'm detail-oriented, too. I like that," she shot back quickly.

"Aww yeah?" I licked my chops shamelessly.

Lisa lowers her tone to nearly a whisper, "Definitely."

"Well, I'm listening."

"I mean I'm just saying…in a good *and* bad way," she continued, explaining her stance. "You bad because you got that power of persuasion. But it can be good for somebody who *wants* to be persuaded."

"Persuasion huh?" I let out another chuckle. She was making this too easy.

"Lawd yes!" she exclaimed. "Like you just 'told' me to give you my number, like you just knew I was gon give it to you."

"Well you *did,* didn't you?" I arrogantly reminded her.

"Yeah, see that's what I'm saying. That confidence…"

"And that's good?" I grinned.

"Bitches love confidence," she confirms seductively.

"So, what about *you*? You said 'it's good for somebody tryna be persuaded'. What you tryna do?" I wanted to know.

"I mean duh nigga, I gave you my number," Lisa said matter-of-factly. "We on the phone, right?"

"Yeah you right, sassy frass," I bit my lip.

"What did you call me?" she asked. "Sassy?"

"Yea…yo sassy ass. I mean you got that same power," I clarified. "I was tryna *text* and you told me to *call*….so I called. Who's the real persuader?"

Lisa started laughing playfully, "You silly!!"

"I'm just saying…"

Lisa's voice lowered, as she spoke with mischief, "Well, I just told you to call me cuz I just got out the shower. My hands are occupied."

"Occupied???" I repeated, full of intrigue.

Ok, let's stop here for a second. This little bitch is

32

obviously throwing the bait out there, I mean I been in the game long enough to pick up on the 'code'. I pause though, cuz I gotta talk to my conscience, at least for shits and giggles.

Lisa is so young...so precious. I mean – she ain't no saint, I can tell from our inboxes and convo that she is definitely a member of *Club Fucking*. But I'm in my prime. I'm on some for real masked monster shit...while she's just getting started in the world. She's not quite 20...my 20s are behind me now. I know it's not fair. Lisa is no match for a nigga of my stature.

But I'm out for blood...

So, she tells me about how her hands are occupied because she's fresh out the shower, lotioning up. Of course, I know there's more to it than that and I probe deeper...on my creep flow. But Lisa isn't shaken or embarrassed. She *wants* me to probe. She goes on to tell me how she plays with her pussy every time she gets out the shower. In fact, that's just one of the *many* times she rubs one out during the day. She has to have at least six rub out sessions per day.

SIX. Per day.

Whoa – ok so 'why 6 a day, lil mama?' I mean I know *why*...obviously she's a freak and loves to cum. I can relate. Who can't? But she's telling me how she can't function or move forward throughout the day unless she busts 6 nuts when it's all said and done. That's a lot, even for a freak.

33

This shit is turning me on something serious, though…my dick is now throbbing uncontrollably in my plaid shorts. Lisa seems to know it too…as she's now lowered her voice as she talks to me. I'm asking her why she ain't getting no dick if she likes to cum so often…and she gives me the typical spill about how she ain't got nobody she's feeling or kicking it with like that right now.

"Ok, perfect. Go in for the kill, Holly…"

"Maaaaan…I don't believe that shit," I decided aloud. "You too muthafuckin bad to be playing with that pussy all the time on yo own like dat."

"I mean, it's cool. Like I said, I *like* touching my shit. I like to cum," she sounded sexy as fuck.

"Damn, so you playing with it *now*???" my eyes widened at the thought.

Lisa could tell she had me on edge, as she whispered softly, "Yes."

"Shit. *You* bad," I told her, giving her the much-earned spotlight.

"Whaaaat?" Lisa whined. "I tried to tell you. I can't help it…"

"Nah, I like dat shit," I wanted her to know. "I like to watch. I like to listen."

So now she's on the phone with me, masturbating

and enjoying the shit like I'm not even there…in her zone, in her element. I'm listening to this shit with a dropped jaw and stiffy outta this world. Her breathing gets deeper, she's moaning. Not loud…but low and seductive. Her voice is so fuckin' sexy…this bitch needs to be on a sex line or some shit. I'm egging her on…asking her how wet it is, telling her to taste it for me. She's all into this shit. We having some serious phone sex – only I'm just 'watching'…

"Damn, how it taste?" I asked, sounding like a phone-sex operator.

Lisa moaned into the phone, "Hmmmm, I taste good daddy…sweet like *honey*."

"I like honey. Damn, I wanna taste that shit."

"Hmmmm," she moans again, this time louder. "I want you to, too…"

I could feel my dick moving, "Shit, you lucky I ain't there right now!"

Lisa lets out another soft moan, "*Lucky*? Nah nigga. *You* lucky…"

"Nah *YOU* lucky!" I replied passionately. "I'm telling you…you just don't know…"

"Well, let me *know* then, HoLLy," she challenged in between moans. "Hmmmm. Let me know…"

35

The whole shit is getting so intense, I'm thinking of pulling my dick out in the parking lot and getting some mutual action in. I've never done no shit like this before...I'm the type that'll pull up on you and be ready to go. If we were texting or instant messaging it'd be different, but I can't handle hearing ya *voice* on the other end on some playing-wit-it shit. I'm tempted to pull off in Shay's car and be outside Lisa's spot in a hop, step, and jump. But I know that can't happen...so my next urge is to play along and jack it off with her. But damn...I'm on some hot shit outside my ex's spot. In her car. And her roommate can pull up at any moment.

We keep talking, and she's started to moan louder – like real loud – and I'm wondering who she stays with. She's honestly young enough to still be at Mom's. But damn, if Mama is in the other room when *this* shit is going on...geeeezus. This is wild.

Lisa sounds like she's getting fucked on the other end...and she's not being shy about it, "Oh my god I'm 'bout to cummm...."

Damn...

She's moaning like a nymph in my ear, and she sounds so *good*. I can't help but grab my dick as she talks me through it...screaming obscenities as her body shakes uncontrollably. She lets one go all over her fingers...with one final high-pitched moan.

"Dude. I need to fuck this chick if it's the last thing I do in life..."

36

"Me and you both, nigga," my **beast** agrees.

"You good?" I finally asked after a few seconds of silence.

"Hmmm, yes. I'm hella good," she mumbles, trying to get herself together.

"Damn, you got me over here like...damn," my voice cracks as I try to snap back to reality myself.

"I'm sorry, baby. I feel bad now," she told me.

"Why, what you mean? Why you feel bad?"

Lisa giggled, "I don't know...you know how you feel dirty right after you nut?"

"Yeah yeah...I can dig it," I could relate. After you cum, you instantly feel disgusted. "But it's all good. Don't feel bad. I like dat shit...you got me curious."

"Aww yeah?" she asked playfully. "What you curious about Mr. HoLLyRod...?"

"I mean, you seem like you on my level," I explained. "I wanna know what all you into."

She hesitates at first, telling me she's not sure how much she wants to tell me. And I tell her that I'll go first so she knows I'm not the amateur by far. I tell her how I'm used to wild, freaky sex. How my ex was bisexual and how we used to have orgies and *ménages* and I used to watch her with chicks.

"Damn, really?" she sounded shocked. "Hmmm…I like chicks too…"

"Damn…for real???"

I'm not as surprised as I sound…I mean at this point, that lifelong fantasy of mine had become the norm. The girl-on-girl culture was mainstream popular, and by 2009, I'd had plenty of experiences in that arena. Plenty…but yet not nearly *enough*. This Lisa chick is turning me on like a muhfucka, and I've gotta get belligerent with this girl.

"So where you at now?" she curiously wondered.

"Shit still in traffic, I pulled over to talk to you. You gon have me crashing out here," I told her no lies.

"Nah I ain't tryna make you crash baby," Lisa said, sounding like she was cheesing from ear to ear.

As she says that, a pair of headlights turn into the lot and shine right at me – and I'm temporarily blinded. The black car pulls up beside me…and I instantly recognize the person in it.

Panicking, without hesitation, I snapped, "Aye lemme call you back real quick…"

Noticeably disappointed, Lisa starts pouting in protest, "Noooo…why????"

*   *   *   *   *

5

"Nah, this cop just got behind me. I'ma hit you back," I lied, in desperate need of the perfect excuse.

"Ok ok," she let her guard down, and I wasn't sure if she believed me. "Talk to you later."

Whether Lisa believed me or not, I hung up quickly and got out the car before Kris noticed I was on the phone. I wasn't near ready to hang up, but rules are rules. Playing it smooth, I walked Kris to the building door – telling her how it was such a coincidence we 'pulled up' back-to-back. Then we went inside to greet Shay, and the three of us watched movies to end the night.

"I can't fuckin' wait 'til my car is running again. This shit is for the birds."

*   *   *   *   *

So fast forward to the weekend. I get my car fixed, and now I'm a free man. The repairs take 'til late Saturday night, so I hit Lisa up Sunday afternoon to see what she's up to. For whatever reason, she's busy during the day but tells me we can hang out later that night. AND…she has her own place.

"A young tender, staying alone...with a 6-Times-A-Day habit? Jackpot, HoLLy!"

Later works just fine for me, that'll give me time to see Shay for a lil bit during the day. If Lisa wanted later, later was perfect...

Only later turned into *much later.*

We finally hook up around booty call hours...but nothing sexual happens. We talk, we fall asleep, we cuddle. I wake up in the middle of the night in my freak mode, and she stops me once I try to touch the pussy. She lets me caress and squeeze her ass...and believe me, with how epic Lisa's ass is, that woulda been more than enough for most niggaz. But a nigga like *me* is used to a different standard. For a nigga like me to be laying up with a bitch who lives in my sister's enemies hood was stupid to begin with. The fact that we ain't even fuck left me beyond frustrated.

So, after that first sleepover with Lisa, my first thought was to never talk to her again. Ain't nobody got time for all'at – bitch how you go from playing with ya pussy the first time we talk on the phone...to telling me you 'not ready' when I get there?

"Hell nah. Bitch I'm HoLLyRod..."

That attitude lasted maybe two days. She still had my intrigue, there was no doubt about that. I couldn't give up that easily, regardless of my recent track record with other situations or where Big Booty Lisa lived, I couldn't let this go. So, I end up hitting her up again via text a couple days later.

The conversations continue to take sexual detours. I start to gather that Lisa likes my freaky mind...she likes how I can openly talk dirty to her. She loves how she can be free with me, and how natural our sexting flows. She insists that she doesn't get as explicit with anyone else, and she's hella turned on by it.

So why the hell she ain't let me fuck that first night?

Weeks pass. End of September now and I'm still on the hunt. I mean, let me be frank...I'm not putting any real *effort* into it. I'm not offering to take her out or spend some money...hell I'm not even showing much interest in getting to *know* her – as a person. Our conversations are simple. Small talk – and then sex. And we only talk every few days, here and there. She knows I want it...I express this openly, but I ain't being extra thirsty about it. On her end, she's not being extra slutty about it. I mean we talk dirty; we stay on some freaky shit. But so far she ain't told me to pull up, and I'm less than 15 minutes from her.

Well one night, we texting right around the start of quiet-storm hours...and I ask her when I'ma see her again.

LISA: "Idk...when u wanna see me again?"

ME: "Shit...now."

LISA: "Lol...like right now? Boy u crazy..."

ME: "Yea...but I'm serious tho..."

LISA: "My ppl over here..."

"Damn. Just my luck!"

"Relax HoLLy. Just ease up a bit...don't seem too anxious."

ME: "Damn ok. Well nvm then..."

LISA: "Why u say nvm? Don't give up that easy."

"See, what I tell you? Here we go..."

"Hell yeah! All she gotta do is say the word and it's on."

"Out for blood, my nigga..."

ME: "Oh, well u tell me. I'm wit whatever."

And then, before she replies…I send another:

ME: "I'll come get u if u want and u come over here…"

She hits me back and tells me she can't come to my spot; she gotta finish packing for her trip tomorrow. She going out of town with her family, and she got some cousins at her place tonight. She wants me to come over, because she misses me too…but she don't want folks all in her business.

I'd rather her come to my spot, but I'm at the point where I'll take the risk of being in her neighborhood without a second thought. So I'm putting in my case, telling her it's all good…I'll be quiet if we chill at her place. She doesn't take me seriously, and knows I'm just saying whatever to get her to agree. But that actually makes her *want* to agree. And so, she does…sending me darting out of my building and to my car in the blink of an eye.

She meets me at the side door like last time, and we ride the elevator up to her floor. She's in some small gym shorts and a *Hello Kitty* pajama shirt, hair tied up in a scarf.

"Don't look at my head!!" she cried out, trying to cover up. "Stoppp…"

"Whaaat?" I smiled. "It's wrapped up, quit acting like that."

45

I pull her closer to me in the elevator and wrap my arms around her waist, cuffing ass with both hands. It's so soft…damn. She hugs me tightly, her head in my chest.

"Dang, you act like you happy to see me," I said, referring to how she held me.

"I ammm…." Lisa agreed, squeezing even tighter.

Ok, so we get to the 5th floor…and start walking down the hall to her apartment. I'm just a step behind her – watching her ass flex as she struts. Lisa got a mean ass walk. I don't know how a bitch this thick can have a switch so synchronized, but she's definitely pulling it off. My dick is jumping in my sweats…I try to play it off as she turns her head around my way.

"Quit looking at it," she said, 'fake' covering it up and blushing. But I can't help it, and she knows it.

We get to the apartment, and she's wuttin' lying – it's a household full of folks in this muhfucka. I get a couple of curious glances from the living room as Lisa walks me right to her bedroom, which is only a few feet from the front door opposite the kitchen. She creeps in slowly, shutting the door behind her. I could still hear her cousins through the wall, in the other room watching a movie. The walls are super thin.

She's got a bunch of clothes on her bed, a suitcase at the foot. After she clears the mattress off, Lisa turns the volume up on the radio sitting to the right side of the bed. I take a seat on the far-left side near the window…freeing

46

my gun from my waist and sliding it under the railing.

Lisa doesn't see me – she's playing *Beyoncé 'Ego'* off the *Sasha Fierce* joint, in her zone as she packs a few things away. I scoot closer towards the middle of the bed, pulling out my phone to kill time, "You got a *Twitter* yet?"

"No!" she responds quickly. "I don't know how to use that shit. I be confused."

We have a laugh. Lots of people say that about *Twitter* but I tell her it's the new thing and she should get one. She's telling me about this trip with her family to southeast Missouri that she really isn't looking forward to going on tomorrow.

By now, another *Beyoncé* song is playing...but it's the '*Upgrade U*' track with *Jay-Z*. I'm almost certain that song was on her last album before *Sasha Fierce,* but I could be wrong. I'm not a *Bey* fan like that so whatever. Maybe it was a *Beyoncé* mixed CD. At any rate, now she's walking around the room looking like she ready to turn it in – putting things away, and then locking her door.

When she hits the light, I tell her I'm taking my sweatpants off, and she says, "Ok, that's cool – I'm sleeping in my panties anyway."

So now we in the bed. I'm in boxer briefs and a tank top. She's backs her ass up on me almost immediately, and I pull her in as close as I can. I know she can feel my **wooD** poking her. I start kissing the back of her neck, and now she's grinding her hips to the music. My hands fall to

47

her breasts...and I start grabbing them through her shirt.
She lifts up after a few seconds and starts to pull her shirt
over her head. My dick tries to burst through my pants to
help her get undressed.

She's laying in her panties next to me now – nothing
else. She turns to face me, and our eyes lock in the
darkness. Without saying a word, we both reach for each
other and crawl closer. I lean in and snatch at her bottom
lip with my teeth...gently tugging before I start kissing her
softly. She pulls away after a couple of seconds...and now
her hands are grabbing my dick under the sheets. I throw
my head back in pleasure...she's got just the right amount
of grip. I'm loving it. She loves that I'm loving it, taking
her other hand to lift up my wife-beater...and then kissing
my chest as she jacks me.

I'm starting to get hot, breathing faster with every
stroke. My **wooD** is so *hard*...I mean like virgin-teenager
hard. The whole scene takes me back to high school
days...making out, not going all the way. There's a certain
erotica to having restrictions, whether involuntary or not.
This is starting to prove true for me at this moment, the
buildup and anticipation has just made me want her even
more.

"But enough is enough," says the beast.

I move in closer and start sucking her nipples.
They're small, but nice...and they harden as soon as my
tongue makes contact. She moans softly, it makes my dick
jump in her hand. My hands are rubbing her arm and
back, slightly scratching and digging my nails into her skin.

She's staring at me, biting her lip.

We lock eyes again and start kissing. This time, I reach down with my right hand...tracing the top of her panty line with my index finger. It's warm down there...really warm. My fingers crawl underneath and make their way down to her lips...but not before finding a pool of juice guarding the gate. She's so wet. I start rubbing her clit, very gently. Slowly.

"Hmmmm...you see how wet I am?" she groans. "Don't stop..."

I take my fingers out her panties and do just that – stop. She gasps in shock, and I smile...taking my two fingers to my mouth to get a taste. This drives her crazy. "You so nasty," she whispers.

"I know," I lowered my eyes, biting my bottom lip. Then I start rubbing her pussy again, and she's squeezing my dick. I can feel her pussy throbbing. I'm only rubbing her clit though, I don't wanna stick a finger in just yet...

Lisa has other plans however, as she puts her hand on mine, guiding my index finger inside of her...

*　　*　　*　　*　　*

6

The masturbation session is getting intense. I'm really working her cat now…with one finger, touching her in ways she's never been touched.

She can't take it no more. Letting go of my dick, she reaches for a pillow, covering her face to keep her moans muffled. It actually works, now I can barely hear her. Her pussy is clenching around my finger, I can't believe how tight she is. If she's this tight around my 1 finger…she's gonna be hella snug on this dick.

She grabs my arm, and I can tell she's cummin' on my finger now. I imagine her biting the pillow as she starts to shake, legs squeezed together tightly as I keep rubbing.

After she calms down…I pull away, whispering her name, "Lisa…"

"Yeah…?" she responds, in between sexy moans.

"Lemme get it…" I demanded sensually.

She moans again, I'm still touching her pussy. She

thrusts upwards, matching my finger motion as she gasps, "I can't…"

"Why nottt?" my eyes widened.

Lisa's squirms and her voice gets whiny again, "Becaaaauuuuuse……my cousins gon hear me…"

"No dey not," I claimed, trying to convince myself more than her.

"Oh but, yes they are," the beast whispers in my head.

"Yes they will!" Lisa squeals, as if she could hear my inner voice. "I'ma be loud…"

Gotdammit…this can't be happening again. She's gonna give me blue balls. Her kitty is dripping…I mean it's doing everything short of screaming at me. I know she wants it. But I mean, she's got the perfect excuse with her little cousins in the next room. This is real torture. I groan in agony and frustration…and try to pull away, but she grabs for my dick again, squeezing and stroking, "I'm sorry baby, I want it too. Soon as I get back in town, I got u. For real."

She's whispering to me, telling me how bad she wants to feel this dick in her, how wet she is just thinking about it. I'm mad as fuck…but she sounds so sexy and I'm so horny, I let her keep jackin' my dick until I bust a loooong, thick nut on her hand. She keeps stroking, making sure she drains me before getting up to look for a towel. After she wipes her hands clean, she then comes and cleans me up, patting my dick and balls gently. With a wet kiss on the lips, she tells me one more time before we go to sleep, "When I get back, I got you…"

Voices in my head started yelling in frustration.

"Another fuckin' strikeout!!!"

"Is this shit even worth all this waiting? What the fuck yo!!! Something's gotta give."

"You know what we gotta do, HoLLy. Fuck it."

*   *   *   *   *

I don't talk to Lisa 'til she comes back. I'm feeling some type of way…on my *HoLLyShit*.

That weekend, I go to *Club Dallas* with my niggaz to get *HoLLyBeLLigerent* – a different level of bafoolery and dedication to going hard. We drank a fifth of *Henny Priv* in the car and errbody, including me, popped at least one *X* *pill.*

It's not a game…

Running with a bunch of street niggaz and music industry affiliates had started to go to my head. I'm the nigga in the club that will grab your ass, wait for you to turn around, and tell you I did it. I expect you to tell me to do it again, once you see it was me. Don't try to dance with me unless we freaking. If I buy you a drink, I'm tryna fuck…if you smile at me twice and ask me personal shit – I'm tryna fuck. I'll warn you, *'Aye look, you keep talking to me, I'ma wanna fuck soooo….'*

So anyway, this little redbone slim bitch in a tan skirt gets the warning and doesn't take heed to it. She's all over me at the bar – telling me how she's been obsessed with me since she saw me on the news at my sister Ronnie's trial. She may not have used the word *'obsessed'*, but the bitch definitely was on a nigga's dick.

Well the bitch – damn I don't wanna keep calling the bitch 'bitch' – that's so **belligerent**. Let's call her a name not close to her real name. Ok, let's call this bitch **Cherry**.

So Cherry is a fan. She's been warned, and she's still damn near in my lap as I sit at the bar. I tell her she's coming back to the *Boom Boom Room* with me, referring to my downtown apartment. She tells me she's down, but there's two issues: she drove and her friend rode with her…and she don't have much time after the club cuz she live with her dude.

"Cool, just tell her to bring her friend, HoLLy. Simple."

She tells me the friend ain't tryna fuck me. I tell her I got nice couches and we won't take much time, maybe 45 minutes to an hour. She can order *Denny's* or *Town Topic* on the way home and tell her man they went to get food.

"Hell, bitch go get some **Chubby's** *for all I give a fuck — just meet me downtown so we can do this."*

Aight so Cherry comes to the **Boom Boom Room** with her chocolate friend. I tell the friend she can pick a couch and I got cable so she can watch whatever she wants. I hand her a blanket in case she gets cold. Then I explain to her how I'm gonna be in the back fucking the ape shit outta Cherry, and she might hear us. But it won't be because I'm tryna show off, I tell her, and she can turn the tv up if she needs to.

Now at this point, her and Cherry are laughing, not knowing whether to take me seriously…but I'm not fucking around. I walk Cherry to the back, out for blood.

So about three and a half hours later, Cherry decides she's had enough and should check on her friend and get home to her man.

PAUSE

I know what y'all thinking. Different story though. Another episode, another time. Let's stick to Lisa, she's the real co-star of this story. But **Cherry** *is relevant. Here's why…*

Now it's the *following* weekend, and Cherry is texting me – wanting to come over after work. She said she gets off at 1am and she doesn't have to go home immediately. This bitch goes on to tell me about how wild it was when we got down the week before, how her man almost choked her out cuz he saw my handprints on her ass. I'm tripping off the fact that I don't remember roughing her up like that – I mean, *prints?!?!*

Ok anyway. *I'm still out for blood*...so I'm like, cool – I'll wait for Cherry to get off.

So now I'm at the *Boom Boom Room* setting up shop. Changing my sheets, straightening shit up, counting my condoms in my various stash spots. I take my shower early...around 10:45...so I can sip and blow and let my Ginseng kick in. As I'm getting out the shower, I get a text out the blue from Lisa.

LISA: "Hey what u doing?"

I debate on whether or not to even text her back, I mean – I'm back feeling real *HoLLy* right now. But then I remember that donkey ass Lisa got...and I decide she owes me some pussy anyway so I can at least hit her back.

ME: "Just got out the shower. Wassup?"

LISA: "Why didn't you wait on me?"

ME: "Lol...how long am I supposed to **wait?**"

LISA: "Lol oh u got jokes?"

ME: "Lol I'm saying how long was I supposed to wait? I had to take a shower..."

LISA: "Ok. Are you coming to see me?"

ME: "??? When?"

LISA: "Tonight?"

*   *   *   *   *

7

My options are simple. I got some '*sure pussy*' on the way that I can get with no hassle. Or I can try my luck again with *Lisa*, who unofficially is becoming a real tease...

"Fuck it. You know the rules, HoLLy."

Errbody knows that rule about new pussy. And I can't really think straight when I think about **LisAss**. So, I tell her I'll be on my way in a minute. New pussy is new pussy.

Fifteen minutes later, I'm high as hell and in route, ready to let loose. I get to Lisa's gated lot just before midnight, she texts me and tells me to enter the building through the front this time. After I check in with security and get on the elevator, I finally get a reply from Cherry about me canceling our rendezvous. She says she's ok with some other time.

"Cool. We got bigger ass to deal with tonight."

Lisa opens the door in her bathrobe. She's been drinking, you can see it in her face. Her robe is hanging open and I notice that she's ass naked underneath. The whole apartment is dark, except for the candles lit in her room, which is where she immediately takes me. I'm following close behind her; I can see the drops of water on the back of her neck from being fresh out the shower.

I lick my lips.

Soon as I hit the room...I start stripping. It doesn't take me long – jacket, tank-top, and sweats are on the floor covering up my gun within seconds. Lisa doesn't see me get naked, she has her back turned – lighting another candle on her dresser. I walk up on her, dick standing up and swinging. She turns around just as I get to her, her thick thigh bumping into my **wooD**, "Damn, HoLLy. You ready, huh?"

"Yeah, come on," I replied immediately. Ready was an understatement.

Her robe hits the floor and for the first time, she's standing in front of me naked – albeit in a candlelit room. But I can see just fine...her body is *right*. Her tits ain't huge, but that made her upper torso compliment her curvy bottom half. Man...she was so fuckin' curvy. Her stomach and waistline, much smaller than expected for an ass that's gotta be 44 inches. I mean dude...I wish I could post her pic with this story so y'all can see it's not just the GG talking. Lisa had the perfect natural build – the type of shape most these girls out here getting body surgery to have.

I turn her around, holding her hand above her head. I wanna see her twirl slowly so I can appreciate the scenery. She's looking me up and down with bedroom eyes as she spins, and then steps toward her bed. She lays on her back, and I climb up towards her...both my hands gripping her thighs.

"Lay back," I demanded mannishly. "Hold yo legs up."

Neither of us hesitate. I rub my left hand across her clit...and then down to her ass, squeezing and grabbing her from underneath. Then I lift her up and bring her crotch up to my face...tongue out and mouth wide. She yells *'ohhh yes'* in satisfaction as I take her whole pussy in my mouth, suction around the lips...tongue circling her clit. She can't take this shit...she pushes me away.

"Fuck that!" I aggressively shouted out. "Bring yo ass here, quit running..."

I pin her legs down with my forearms and lay into her shit...holding her firmly in place as I suck at her juices. Drooling and slurping, I start shaking my head in it while I taste her. She's squirming and jerking – we're both twisting as my arms wrestle with her big, strong legs. She's trying to find leverage but failing miserably.

See when I'm giving face, it's quite the gift to receive. She's desperately searching for that angle where she can handle it, moving her hips and trying to anticipate which way my tongue will bully her next. This shit turns me on...my dick is pulsating against her mattress.

Her moaning and sounds of ecstasy don't have to be

restricted tonight, and she's relishing in this...her voice drowning out the music pouring out her speakers. I didn't even realize she had the music playing until I couldn't hear it momentarily. As I get lost in this oral masterpiece of a performance, I start imagining in my head all the different positions I'm gonna fuck this girl in. Both my hands grab her waist, face still in it...and she's meeting my offense now with some serious hip action. She knows how to get head. I'm loving this shit.

Lisa then takes my skull in both hands and pushes me down in it...and I'm sucking her clitoris again with conviction. I know she gon bust. I want her to cum all on my chin, I wanna taste every drop of the extra wetness I know is coming. I can feel it building up...and I take two fingers...sliding them in easily. It's so slippery. But the fit is tight; her pussy almost hurts my two fingers...even more so when she starts clenching up. Her back lifted upwards...ass still on the bed, "Oh my god HoLLy, I'm bout t...."

"Mmmm hmmm...come on," I smacked my lips. "Let that shit out..."

"Right ther...don't stahp," she squirms, twisting and jerking to my fingers, "Hmmmm...shiiiiit!!! Don't stop bab...eee...fuck!"

I'm fingering her with just one finger now, and you can hear the juices throughout the room, dripping and splashing all over my chin and neck. She's cummin *hard*...I mean *HARD*.

And I keep going…

She tries to stop me. But I keep licking away, running my tongue up her slit…sticking it into the clit hood in stride.

She's pushing me away again. And I'm still destroying my meal…smacking my food like I have no manners…

Lisa manages to find her voice again, "HoLL…."

"Hmmmmmm," with her clit still in my mouth, I responded with only a moan.

"HoLLy," she mumbles again, this time more distinctively.

"Mmmm hmmmm," I moaned again with a drenched face.

"HoLLy, boo," she groaned with urgency. "Come on…"

I sit up now, rubbing her legs as I look at her face in the dark. She's staring at me, panting, "You got a condom???"

"Wait. Did I forget to bring…"

63

"Nigga, I know damn well you better have a condom, HoLLy. Quit playing bro!"

"Fuuuuck!!!"

*   *   *   *   *

8

I hop up and reach for my sweats…but I already know before I find them.

"Bro, how you let me forget the condoms, bro???" I blame my beast.

"Nigga, you never forget the rubbers, nigga! Come on dawg…you gotta be joking!"

The look of disappointment on my face said it all, "Damn, baby…"

"You didn't bring no condoms???" Lisa can't believe it.

"I was rushing out the door," I started explaining, knowing I fucked up majorly.

"Fuuuuuuck nah!!!!" she yelled out.

"Maaaaan…this some bullshit!!" I planted my right hand on the bed, sitting up straighter.

"Clearly!!!" Lisa is noticeably upset. "Come on now, you knew you was getting some pussy!!!"

67

I shook my head, disgusted at myself, "I know, I just...man. I'll go get some..."

"No. It's ok, I don't want you to leave," she expressed softly.

"No, it's not ok, I can't fuck you raw," I sighed. "I can just run to the gas station real quick."

"No, you most definitely cannot fuck me without a condom, you right," Lisa co-signed. "But no – I don't want you to leave right now. It's ok, HoLLy."

Then she pulls the cover up and over us, "We can just do it next time. Lay down..."

"FUCK ME MAN!!!"

How the fuck did I forget the damn condoms?!?!?!? I must have at least 30 Magnums spread all over my apartment. Mainly under my mattress and on my nightstand...but I've got 'em stashed in the couches and a couple of other key places where it 'could go down'. I mean dude, I *keep* condoms! Tax-free at that! I get the 36-pack from *WallyWorld* – straight charged to my Health Spending Account. There is never an excuse for me not having condoms on me. And especially *knowing* I been tryna bag this chick for about a month and a half now.

Is this a sign?

For all this trouble, maybe Lisa ain't meant to be a success story. Could that be the case? I hated to think so…even after that fumble of a night.

* * * * *

I didn't see Lisa again until Halloween weekend, and this time our hook-up went quite different.

My one-year lease was ending in my new downtown apartment and I was moving to a loft a few blocks away. After a long week of packing, I was long overdue for a break.

So anyway, yeah – it's Halloween weekend, and I wanna go see *Paranormal Activity*. I ain't wanna go alone though, I'll wait 'til it comes out on DVD before I do that. Fuck that – I ain't crazy. I need a movie date.

But the first problem is…I rarely go on dates or in public with a chick. The second problem is, me and Shay have been arguing over the last week about me fucking Kris while Shay was sleep.

Shay is the only chick I would consider taking anywhere in public and that's not happening while we beefing.

So, I'm going through my options now that the movies is out of the question with my main chick. I need some hoe time either way, so I might as well see what my other hoes are doing tonight.

Cherry is at work as usual, and she gets off too damn late. I need to be entertained way sooner than creep hours tonight.

Jayla – this is another lil freak I met at *Club Dallas*. But she always wanna drink and the hoe is too talkative. I mean once we fucking, this lil bitch is *off* the chain. Her 5'10" frame made for a flexible and creative session every time. But tonight, I ain't feeling like dealing with a drunk slut. And besides...I haven't really talked to her for real since I hooked back up with Sashé over the summer. So, Jayla still got a major attitude about me dealing with my ex again.

Amy – my lil white bitch in the Burg. Another Jayla-like scenario, though. This bitch loves to pop pills and get wasted – she goes hard every time. I'm tempted because I can always get her to sell some pussy for me when I'm with her. But at the same time, I don't feel like cleaning loose strands up all day the next morning. The lil bitch hair be shedding. Nah, not tonight.

Suga – I met Suga B at the studio almost two weeks ago. Now I could tell this girl was dangerous from jump. But her short and thick frame mixed with chocolate skin got the better of me, and we've fucked a couple of times already, so I know what I'm getting with her ass. But, that's also the problem – I know what I'm getting with Sug. This bitch is a *squirter*. I'd never had a squirter before linking up with Sug, and it honestly caught me so off guard that I haven't figured out how to react to it yet. But now that I've had my face sprayed – I think I might be lowkey obsessed with it, which kind of scares me. And I mean again, I'm not tryna clean up all day tomorrow and

70

if Sug comes through, she's gonna drench my whole apartment.

This is where I start to process the third and biggest problem. My rebuilt roster is solid, but it's nowhere near as structured as it used to be before I left Kells for Sashé. Back in those days when my creeping was fulltime, my roster was the perfect formula for *The Art of Cheating*. A good lineup includes your main chick, your side chick, and if you're advanced in the game – a third regular reserve. Most cheaters will deal with more than three chicks at once, but one should have no more than three *main* focal points. Any extras are classified as roster-fillers…merely backup plans you can sometimes rely on.

The days of having a perfect roster were behind me now. Even though Sashé was wearing the main chick crown again by default, I was still technically single, and this new lineup was a bunch of extras at best. I just wasn't feeling none of these hoes like that to the point where it was a no-brainer on which one to hit up on a night like this.

So that brings us back to *Lisa*. We still haven't fucked, so I can't really consider her on my roster yet. And normally I'd never consider asking someone I ain't smashed yet on a date. But I really wanna see this movie, so fuck it.

I decide to hit her up and see if she wanna catch a flick with a nigga. Of course, she does.

But on the way to the theater, she's telling me how

she doesn't wanna see the *Paranormal* joint. I'm a little annoyed at first, but I hear her out. So, we end up getting into this little convo about the supernatural and spirit world and what not – you know, real classic stoner talk. And I'm kinda digging the vibe so I ultimately agree to see whatever she wants to see. Lisa's been having her way with me all this time anyway, right?

But then the chick picks *This Is It*...the *Michael Jackson* joint.

Alright – so now I'm contemplating again. I mean – don't get me wrong...I'm a huge *MJ* fan. It's just not the type of time I was on tonight and I've been through enough nights of bafoolery with Lisa. So if I sit through this shit – I'ma really be pissed if I don't fuck yet again. Not only pissed...I mean my very legacy could depend on how this shit pans out.

Then I remember, I'm playing chess...not checkers. Lisa's sexual energy seems like it could be the perfect replacement for Sashé's. I been on the offensive so much that maybe, just *maybe*...that's why I haven't had the upper hand with this whole plan yet. This could actually be a good move, if I play it right.

Turns out, we both fall asleep on the movie...and leave early. We get back to her spot – and I sit in the living room instead of going to the bedroom. We sit around, we talk...hang out. But it's already late, and so I tell her I'ma go ahead and turn it in after about a half hour...and she stops me at the door.

The rumbles of my ~~beast~~ stir up immediately, knowing this is the night it goes down.

The sex is beyond excellent. *Well* worth the wait. This Lisa chick literally was an *animal* once she had some penetration, and she could go multiple rounds. I wake her up at least twice in the middle of the night to go another round...and she's just as energetic each time. A rarity, to say the least. Not only that...she really let me fuck her how I wanted to fuck her. My ~~beast~~ felt right at home – dominant, aggressive, demanding. Once she was bent over and taking back shots...Lisa finally let me have my way with her. She never said *'no'* once...not to anything that night, which is a *major* fucking turn-on for a nymph with control issues.

So, it's all said and done, and we go our separate ways in the early morning. I text her when I make it back home to my apartment filled with half-empty boxes everywhere.

ME: "I made it..."

LISA: "Ok, good. Thanks for last night, I really enjoyed myself."

ME: "Me too, it was well worth the wait..."

LISA: "Yes it was! Thanks for waiting on me lol..."

ME: "Uhm...ok. You're welcome..."

LISA: "So did you **really** wait??"

"Damn...ok, so now she testing the waters a little bit," I mumbled in my head.

"We tell no lies in The Art. Only half-truths."

"Then why do I feel like I wanna tell her the whole truth??" I wondered.

ME: "Well I mean, technically...no. Hell nah lololol..."

LISA: "Smh wooow! At least you're honest lol"

ME: "Lol I mean I'm just saying. I feel like I don't have a reason to lie to u. You asked, so I answered..."

LISA: "Hmmm...damn. Ok – I can respect that. I can't even be mad at that..."

ME: "No you can't be mad period...not after how I made u cum last night! Fuck that lol..."

LISA: "LMBO!!! OK! Whew!!!"

This is the beginning of how Lisa and I developed our unexpected relationship. She rocks with me from that point on, knowing what she gets when dealing with me. Our interactions are mostly sexual...the attraction stays real. But every now and then, she and I have a real conversation or two. Lisa has now started to admire me for my honesty and tendency to keep it real if she asks me my opinion about some shit. I'm kinda digging how I ain't gotta lie to her about everything. For some reason, we just clicked in a weird way. We both knew about others in the picture...but we still got it in when the chance presented itself. It just kind of becomes our thing.

So where does all this lead, you ask? All of this backstory about Big Booty Lisa leads us to the second half of this episode, where Big Booty *Shonne* comes into the picture...

*   *   *   *   *

Fast forward about two years later, and *HoLLyWorld* has done a complete 180. You know it's hard to make a long story short, so bear with me...

When I met Lisa in the summer of 2009, I was out for blood. Mainly because of the Sashé breakup and the *Silent Promise* revenge plot. I was technically single and rebuilding my roster of bitches to terrorize as a coping mechanism. I was jaded, bitter, and fueled by my inner beast, pouring my buried emotions into the music. My

Grandpa Jerry was infamous for intentionally getting different chicks in different cities pregnant…and without acknowledging it, I was starting to proudly carry some of his same energy Pops warned me about.

My belligerent ~~beast~~ wuttin' setting out to create a bunch of bastard kids, but still my sins were headed for the worse. I began disregarding what I knew to be true about the *Son's Curse* as far as unsettled energy and emotion. I had become the epitome of the monster living inside, relying on my arrogant experience with *The Art* to be my defense against any attempt at potential karma.

Heavier drinking and newfound drug habits eventually had me misreading all the signs and interpreting things the way I *wanted* to see them. Pops told me the Curse would always find a way. He said that it would use the universe to warn me…energy from the past would reappear to force me to make better decisions.

Pops was always right. Even when I refused to see it and swore that I had become untouchable, Pops was right about everything. He always said you can't escape fate.

When I met Lisa, like the rest of the bitches I was fucking with, she was simply food for my ~~beast~~, at a time where no one was to be spared. I needed to get over Sashé, I needed to uncage myself to have the ultimate revenge. There was something about Lisa though, that made me open up a bit with her. We had started to have conversations of substance, conversations that I wuttin' having with anybody else. Even though the both of us were mutually involved with others, there was this unforeseen level of respect and understanding we developed for each other outta nowhere. At some point, for some reason, Lisa's feelings started to matter to me.

The ~~beast~~ didn't like it, and since I couldn't understand it myself no matter how much I tried to make sense of it…I kept Lisa close, but at a distance. The honesty between us coupled with the lack of being judgmental scared the shit outta me. It reminded me too much of what I had before with Sashé the first time around. Because of this…I made it a point to only let Lisa get so close. I was in revenge mode and still on a mission to avoid heartbreak. Out for blood. And I needed to continue feeding off of the sinister and belligerent energy I had become comfortable with. So that's what I did. And in the midst of that, I ended up giving Grandpa Jerry's legacy a new face of audacity.

But the *Curse* is tricky.

Eventually, the same emotional energy and attachment I had been trying to avoid by distancing myself, somehow still found a way to keep coming back around.

I had seen it early on with Lisa and focused on keeping somewhat of a wall up with her. Our chemistry was too effortless, like it had been with Sashé. I knew there was unsettled energy with Shay in the universe, and I knew I had likely amplified it when I took Shay back in with vengeance in my heart. I knew the *Curse* would keep trying to find a way, and since I felt it was apparent that *Lisa* carried that reappearing energy – I thought she was

77

all I needed to worry about.

But when I avoided getting too serious with Lisa, the *Curse* then found another vessel, with a whole *different* chick on my roster that I never saw coming. I dodged a commitment with Lisa no problem, but then I ended up in an even deeper relationship with Suga B, who I had met almost two months after that Lisa photo shoot.

The next two years would flip my world upside down. By 2011, I had moved back to St. Louis and found myself technically single once again, this time in an on-and-off again rollercoaster with Sug. And Sug would end up hurting me way worse than Sashé. This is where we find me in the second half of the story.

In a different city. Still jaded. Out for more blood. And now even more belligerent than before after one of the toughest years of my life.

October 2011

It's fall again…close to around the same time of year when Lisa first gave me the pussy. We still keep in touch, but it's been a minute since we fucked. I mean, we live in different parts of the state now. She been seeing some other nigga for a minute, plus it's getting kinda serious. And since I had been in my own world on some toxic shit with Sug, over the last couple of years, my contact with Lisa had turned minimal.

During this time – I'm real *Twitter*-active. If there was ever a such thing as ***TwitterCool***…I invented that shit. *Twitter* became like my playground…another arena of pure ***belligerence*** and all out ignorance. I tweet what the fuck I want and what I want is usually a bunch of madness and comedy. I was one of the first original troll gawds.

Most of the folks I interacted with via *Twitter* – I ain't know personally. A small pocket of folks I fucked with in real life, but for the most part, my followers or followees were just avatars on the screen. Individuals plugged into a matrix of sorts. So it's like this – when you plugged in the matrix, you in a world that's not real. That's how I always liked to look at it.

Every once in a while, though…you might find somebody in the matrix who you end up in the same room with offline. Well, this is how I met Big Booty *Shonne*.

I had been following this Shonne chick for a minute…though I never really engaged with her. She interacted regularly with some mutual friends from KC, so I guess that's how she ended up on my timeline. One day, I see her tweet some shit about how she loves to cook. I tweet back…and so it begins.

HoLLyDigital: "@ShonneGotSkills well damn, I love to eat – that sounds like a perfect match. Meet me halfway…"

ShonneGotSkills: "@HoLLyDigital hmm I

just might...what you got a taste for?"

Since this could go a variety of different ways...I take this chance to peep out her avi. She was nothing special, just a chick with a young-looking face.

"She throwing the pussy though, HoLLy. You know what time it is," the ~~beast~~ whispers on schedule.

HoLLyDigital: "@ShonneGotSkills don't matter long as it's warm and juicy..."

What happens next is where this story comes full circle. Out of nowhere, I get a tweet from *Lisa's Twitter* profile...directed at both me *and* Shonne.

LusciousLisaaa: "@HoLLyDigital @ShonneGotSkills uhm don't be flirting with my SISTER Rodney!!!"

*   *   *   *   *

S1E3: HoLLy BeLLigerence

9

"Boi ain't no way boi…"

"Hold up nigga, Lisass got a sister??" my ~~beast~~ starts drooling with belligerence.

"Boi ain't no fuckin' way boi!!!"

"Just let it play out, HoLLy."

HoLLyDigital: "@LusciousLisaaa @ShonneGotSkills LOL u betta tell ya sis to quit flirting wit me!"

LusciousLisaaa: "@HoLLyDigital @ShonneGotSkills smh u a mess! Don't play wit me LMBO!!"

Ok so let's pause again for a second. Now again, I ain't talked to Lisa *'like that'* in a minute…but we still cool. Mutual respect is still there and, given the opportunity again, I would fuck her brains out. I mean, we had a cool

83

little history, ya dig? Still though, as close as it felt like we were getting at one point, I had made sure to keep that distance. But this makes me realize I don't know much of anything about Lisa. I know she had other sisters and brothers...but *details*? I barely had any.

So now she's tweeting me telling me to leave her sister alone...and I don't know if this is her real sister or not. In fact, I *automatically* eliminate that as a possibility because this Shonne chick don't look shit like Lisa in the face, other than the fact they both look super young. Hell, they look damn near the same age – how can they be sisters?

This gotta be one of those situations where they *'play sisters'* or grew up around the same people so they consider themselves sisters. Close friends perhaps. Right?

Or maybe not even close at all. I am dealing with some Kansas City chicks – and errbody knows KC is the City of *JEFFIN*. So they might only know each other from around the way and this is prolly one of those **#StopTheJeffinKC** moments...

Right??

Besides, if they was blood sisters...or even cool for that matter...then Shonne wouldn't 'a hopped in my private DM's just minutes after that little exchange...*right?*

ShonneGotSkills: "U can't be talking to me

like that in front of everybody lol!"

HoLLyDigital: "Talking to u like what? Lol I was being good..."

ShonneGotSkills: "Mmm hmm, I been following yo crazy ass! I know better!"

HoLLyDigital: "Girl what u think u know?! Lol...I just be talking shit..."

ShonneGotSkills: "Lol whatever! All that freaky shit u be talking! Yo page is like porn!"

HoLLyDigital: "LMAO! My bad if I offend you...I can't help it..."

ShonneGotSkills: "No offense boo! I like that shit, it's cool!"

HoLLyDigital: "You like that shit huh? Smh..."

ShonneGotSkills: "Hell don't judge me – we grown! Who doesn't like to cum?"

HoLLyDigital: "I can't think of anybody..."

ShonneGotSkills: "Exactly so shut it! Now tell me what u wanna eat..."

HoLLyDigital: "Smh...u know my mind stays in the gutter..."

ShonneGotSkills: "Lol mine too...I wanna hear you say it..."

HoLLyDigital: "Hmmm...Miss ShonneGotSkills you nasty..."

ShonneGotSkills: "Lol I'm a perv...I know. Sue me!"

HoLLyDigital: "Nah no need for that. What u wanna hear me say? I'm a real to-the-point guy. Tell me..."

And so, it begins.

But meanwhile, Lisa isn't the only one who sees the *Twitter* exchange. I then get a call from my nigga *Jaz*, who knows Shonne from around KC. Jaz had been one of my closest friends since we were college roommates before I pledged *Kappa*. He was also deeply involved in my music path as the engineer and owner of the studio I recorded at. We go back years, so it's safe to say this nigga knew me better than most and could tell what I was up to even 300 miles away.

"Bro you 'bout to fuck Shonne," he asks by telling me.

I started laughing hysterically, "Nigga whatchu

talking about brooo?!?!?"

"Yeah nigga!" Jaz was cracking up too now. "I already know!! I seen that shit nigga!"

"Nah bro, I was just talking shit! She started it!" I insisted.

"Nigga I know yo ass!" Jaz wasn't fooled. Cutting his laughs short, he switched gears, "But broooo…*nigga*!"

"Wassup bro?!?!" I could tell that meant he knew something. "Holla at me! You know this chick?"

"Maaaan…*NIGGA!!!*" he emphasized. "Her ass so muhfuckin' fat…"

"You *LYING!!!* Bro don't tell me that!"

"Wait…hol up!" he paused. "You ain't even seen her *ass,* bro?!?!"

"Nah bro, she just hit me on *Twitter,*" I told him. "I don't even know this chick."

That made Jaz super excited, "Awww nigga! Bro that muhfucka so fat! She work downtown bro, I see her all the time."

"Daaaamn...man I gotta see this ass," I licked my lips, drifting off at the thought.

"Nigga look," he snaps back. "I'ma call you when I

get outta this session. We gotta rap!"

"Aight bet, nigga," I ended the call with a smirk.

Damn, so now I'm hella intrigued. My nigga Jaz knows what I like, and I can never have too many fat-ass'd chicks in my life. In fact, now that I'm technically single in St. Louis, I ain't have no **Lisass** type chicks on my roster anymore. In all actuality, with all the bullshit going on with Sug, I barely had a roster anymore at all.

It would be nice to get on some **HoLLy BeLLigerence** again for old time's sake…right?

"Damn right! Nigga, fuck Sug!" my beast was never shy about his distaste for how crazy things had gotten with Suga B.

So, I don't waste no time – I shoot Shonne a message so we can start texting. Right from jump, she's talking my language. She's a lot younger than me though.

"Man, they all are. You know the deal, HoLLy."

"Every man deserves a slew of young tenders and is entitled to a young wife in the end," I recited in my head handed-down wisdom from my nigga **Goldie**. Shonne is definitely the ideal age.

But she's also got a couple of kids. Now I don't discriminate against MILFs by any means…I'm just never willing to play stepdaddy. So that really ain't a deal breaker. Most chicks with kids love to cook, like she said.

And like I said, I love to eat. Not just pussy, but real food.

I rarely even go in my kitchen though…and there's never any groceries. As I'm telling her this, she's telling me how that pisses her off and how I need somebody to cook for me. What man in his right mind would disagree?

As the conversation continues, I also try to see if I can get a pic from her in our first text exchange…but she doesn't bite on it. Perhaps she knows I've heard about her booty and now I wanna see. Which couldn't be closer to the truth, so I don't make a big deal out of it. *But*…I do tell her that I have to see what her toes look like before we can keep texting. I gotta at least need to know the bitch keeps her toes right if I'm gonna start having lustful thoughts about her. She finds this hilarious…but sends a toe pic pronto.

"Her toes are gorgeous. Damn."

"Jackpot, nigga!"

Ok, so now I decide I can talk freely. But as soon as I throw a nasty comment out there, Shonne stops me. She says she is addicted to sex and we can't be talking shit with me being so far away. Nice. So we end the exchange there, with me telling her I'll be good for *now*.

So later that day, maybe around 6 or 7 that evening, Jaz hits me back with a *FaceTime* call from the studio...

But when I pick up...it's not *Jaz* on the camera.

It's Big Booty *Shonne*....

*   *   *   *   *

S1E3: HoLLy BeLLigerence

10

I know it's *Shonne*, even though this is the 1st time I've laid eyes on her in life. I semi-recognize the face from *Twitter*…but I know Jaz and I just talked earlier about this chick and it would only make sense if it's her calling from his device.

She's smiling, sitting in the control room in one of the chairs against the wall, behind Jaz's chair. I'd spent enough time at *64111 Studio* to know it like the back of my hand. I hear Jaz – loud and drunk – in the background talking shit to some of his clients in the hallway.

"Well, hey there," I smiled.

"Hi, HoLLy," she responded flirtatiously. "Nice to meet you, HoLLy…"

I chuckled back, "What the hell *you* doing at the studio?"

"I just got off work," she told me. "Jaz wanted me to bring him some food and I owed him lunch soooo…"

"Hmm, I see," I shook my head. "Not even gonna ask!"

"Oh, it's not like that! Jaz is the homie," she promised.

"Yeah I know, that's my nigga," I knew it was innocent. "Wassup tho? Lemme get a look at you."

Just then, Jaz comes in the room…drunk and belligerent. For the record, I've always believed this nigga was always constantly more belligerent than me, but that's a whole different story…some other time. Anyway, he comes in excited – snatching the *iPad* from Shonne, "Yeah boa – I was like, *'lemme **FaceTime** my nigga Rod so he can see what you working with!!'*"

I started laughing, "Bro, you drunk!!!"

"Man!" Jaz couldn't disagree. "Them niggaz brought another pint of Henn…but I'm good nigga! Aye girl – stand up, you know my nigga wanna see that shit!!!"

I almost can't believe how **belligerent** this nigga is being right now…but I'm used to it after fifteen years of friendship. However, the way Shonne stands up immediately from his demand does throw me completely off square. I mean, she gets right up, turning around while Jaz plays camera man. All to give me a good peek at the booty.

And *man*. Dat muhfucka *super fat*! I'm talking a real nice apple-bottom and a *really* small waist. I can't believe how proportionately shaped this bitch is.

She's not as cute in the face as Lisa…but she's not busted at all. Her hair is kinda short – the same as most hoes' hair without the weave. And her tits look medium sized through her black sleeveless shirt – but I can see her hard nipples.

Damn...

You can tell this chick is a freak by the way she turns around for the camera...giggling at the attention she's getting from *two* belligerent ass niggas.

"Jaz you silly!" she played modest. "Shut up!!!"

"Man...man...*man!!*" Jaz can't contain himself. "Aye Rod boaaaa..."

He hands her the *iPad* and hurries out the room, before he says something he shouldn't. Jaz can be an asshole, but he ain't disrespectful or wild when it comes to females. He leaves that role up to me.

"Damn mama...it's like that?" I asked with playful insinuation.

"Yup. Pretty much," she shot back at me. "You ain't ready!!!"

"Shiiiiit...girl you don't know who you talking to!"

Shonne giggled in jest, "Yeeaaa...you right about that!"

"We gon change that, though," I pressed on.

"Are we though???" she challenged.

"That's what I'm saying. You need to come to St. Louis," I suggested.

"Hmmm," she was hesitant. "I don't knowww...you might be trouble..."

"I *am* trouble," I agreed mischievously. "But...we *grown*."

"*Mmmm hmmm,*" she moaned. "Well, somebody told me I shouldn't mess with you."

I gave a light chuckle, "Now why would somebody tell you that? Who said that??"

"My little sister."

I paused, "Yo little sister?!?! Who is your sister??? How she know me?"

"*Lisa,* nigga!" Shonne snapped back sharply. "You know that's my sister!!!"

"Damn...Lisa is yo sister?? Like...yo *real* sister???"

"Yea...*duh*! I mean...can't you tell???" she asked, looking back at it.

My inner beast was wide awake now, *"Gotdamn right we can tell!! I know I can tell, fuck what HoLLy playing dumb about."*

I had to admit, the amount of booty between these two chicks was phenomenal. Y'all already know about the Legend of **Lisass**. Well Shonne...her ass was but a few inches smaller. She was more petite than Lisa overall...but this bitch was super thick, just like her sister. They were built damn near the same, the genetics behind this shit was amazing.

"Daaaaaaamn. That's crazy," I shook my head.

Shonne grinned and bit her lip, "Yea I'm the *big* sister, boy!"

"Yes, you are," I couldn't disagree. "Damn. Yes, the fuck you are."

Ok, now I gotta get myself together and assess this situation that just presented itself. My immediate first thought was, *"Wow, so Shonne is really Lisa's older sister!"*

"Shoulda known Lisa was dead serious when she said that shit on Twitter. Look at her booty, bruh..."

"But...damn, if Shonne know I fucked her sister...*why would she be talking to me now? What's going on here?"*

"Does she even know?"

"She has to know. She has to," I was sure of it.

"But, why would Lisa tell you not to mess with me?"

my voice interrupted my thoughts.

"You tell me...why *would* she say that?" Shonne raised her eyebrow.

"Uhm...I don't know," I insisted. "I don't know why anybody would say that about me."

"I mean, she told me y'all used to talk. And she said that you really had a good heart, but you only allow most people to see the asshole. So, I shouldn't fuck wit you."

Ok, that makes sense – right? Lisa told her sister we had a thing, and to leave me be...that's what *should* happen in this scenario. But, I wonder what all she told her. I don't know the extent of their relationship. Hell, I don't know what it's like being sisters with anybody. I mean, I got a sister – but a brother/sister relationship is different from a sister/sister thing. *Especially MY* brother-n-sister 'ship. Ronnie ain't ya typical sister.

I do know *women* though. If it's one thing I've learned living with the *Son's Curse* as a student in *The Art of Cheating*, it's the world of females. I know women talk, share details, and put it all out there. It's safe to assume that if there's a woman with two friends...all three of them know each other's business. If a chick confides in only one of those friends because she's 'not as close' to the other one...then that friend who swore to secrecy gon at least tell the other friend in the dark and tell *her* not to tell anybody. That's just **SCIENCE**.

Stay with me here. What I'm saying is – females talk.

And if Lisa and Shonne are blood sisters, then they gotta be closer than *friends* by default. Right? Shonne probably knows *everything*. How I used to fuck Lisa like a porn star…how often we got it in. How she would sneak away from the club across the street from **The Graham Suites** to fuck me and be back before last call for alcohol. I'm sure Shonne knows all'at shit…

"ARE you sure though, nigga?"

Ok. Well, then again, maybe not. How close *are* they? One other thing I've learned about women is that they some devious creatures…much sneakier than any man could ever be. They got them catty streaks. A woman will snake her closest friend over some dick in a heartbeat. I've seen it and proved it.

"But…hold up, Rod — sisters??? Why would sisters be on that type shit?"

"All the shit we've seen though, HoLLy? Mothers fucking the daughter's dude…cousins or even aunties be stealing the dick. These bitches don't care."

"But dawg, I ain't never heard of no shit like this with no sisters. It's gotta be a trick."

"Man, but you deserve this after the year we just had. Just let it play out, HoLLy…"

"Hmm," I licked my chops, sizing big sis up again. "So, how you feel about what Lisa said? You not gon fuck with me?"

"I mean, that's my sister," she half-heartedly reminded me.

"Yeah but...ain't she got something serious going on right now, though?" I threw the rumor mill at her.

"Yeah...that's neither here nor there," she looked down, as if she wanted to leave that alone. "But...like you said, I'm grown. I fuck with who I wanna fuck with. And I wanna fuck with you."

"Maaaaaaan...it's gotta be a trick! Right?"

Just let it play out HoLLy! We deserve this shit..."

*   *   *   *   *

11

"Damn that's wild," I was still taken aback. "Y'all for real blood sisters??"

"Same daddy, different mamas," Shonne explained. But yup..."

"Damn, so what else she tell you?"

"Nothing...don't worry about it. I'm still talking to you, right?" she pointed out. "I told you what I want."

"This is true. So, that mean you coming to visit?" I wondered.

"I just might. Yup," Shonne smiled with her tongue out.

"Yeah," I didn't bother hiding the thirst in my voice. "I think you should."

"Boy, you crazy!" her face lit up. "Ok, I'ma text you. I need to get up outta here."

As she hangs up, my thoughts start going nuts again. This shit gotta be a trick, dude. Ain't no way Shonne 'bout

to gimme the pussy if she know I fucked her younger
sister. That's just...nasty.

Before my beast even says it, I know I'm a nasty
muthafucka. Make no mistake about it...if given the
opportunity, I would fuck this chick. An ass like that is
too hard to pass up.

But I mean...this is Lisa's *sister*. I was out for blood
when I met her. Hell...I'm *still* out for blood and by all
accounts, even more so now. The hunger in my beast has
grown tremendously, and I ain't limited the belligerence in
years.

But I also never had any reason to hurt Lisa. We
remained cool over time, I ain't never been on no bullshit
with her. She knows what I was after at first and she's had
a peek inside my head since then. I know she's doing her
thing with this other cat now, which I can respect. Maybe
I should back off.

"Nigga, you don't owe Lisa shit."

*"Lisa never done nothing to fuck me over bro, come on now. I
ain't that trifling...am I? I wouldn't dare fuck KeLLy's sister if she
threw it at me."*

*"Yeah, but that's Kells, nigga. Lisa nuttin' never yo girl!!! Y'all
barely even talk anymore, bruh. And don't forget you fucked damn near all
of Sashé's friends, nigga. Don't start acting brand new. This some legendary
shit, HoLLy! Stop playing!"*

"Yeah, but Shay *was different. You stop playing, nigga. The*

104

point is — as wild as we been getting, I ain't never fucked no sisters, dawg. It just feels like that should be the safe zone..."

"Lisa don't fall in that safe zone, if there is such a thing! Quit putting her ass on a pedestal! She supposedly in a serious thing with her new guy; you heard the wedding bells rumor nigga. How can she get mad if her sister trying to give it up?"

Why *do* I care if she gets mad? What's the worst that can happen? Lisa hates me forever and refuses to gimme the pussy ever again? I mean the way it looks...I may not get the pussy again *anyway*. She's caked up – and I'm in a different city. Plus...the ~~beast~~ was right. If I somehow pulled this off, this would be one helluva story. It's not every day you get to bang a couple of sisters.

Still...I continue to wrestle with my conscious over this shit. There was something in my gut that just felt like this time would be taking it too far.

*   *   *   *   *

It's later in the week. I'm sipping and hanging out at my frat brother Ricky Rhymes' crib. Ricky lives in St Louis too now, which was lucky for me. Aside from him managing my music career, Rick has also helped me get out of multiple jam ups over the years. Before we got too lit, I decided to tell him about my latest dilemma.

"So, what's the dilemma though, bro?" he asked after I tried to explain again. "Sound like a win-win from my point of view."

"I guess what I'm tripping off of is – I don't wanna be made out to be the bad guy in this shit," I admitted.

Ricky wasn't buying it, "Nigga, you *live* to be the bad guy!!!"

"Yeah, but bro, come on now. What am I supposed to do as far as *Sister A*?" I was torn. "Do I hit her up and tell her *Sister B* is tryna get at me…even though she told her not to?"

"Why would you do that?" Ricky thought I was crazy. "Bro, they sisters. They both prolly already know. But, let's say they don't. Let's say *Sister A* told *Sister B* to not fuck with you. We know that happened for sure. But let's say *Sister B* reaches out anyway and don't tell *Sister A* what she's up to. How is that on YOU?"

I thought about it, "I mean, it's not but…I'm just saying. What if *Sister A* ask me wassup???"

"*Then* you tell her, cuz you don't have nothing to hide. You said you ain't never not told her the truth about whatever she asks, right?"

"Right…for the most part," I confirmed. "If she *asks*, I usually keep it a hunnid with Lisa. I don't know why, but that's just the shit I been on with her."

Ricky rubs his chin, "Ok then, stay consistent. Don't *offer* her the information. But if she asks…you come clean because it's not like you on some snake shit behind her back. You just a nigga tryna fuck a bitch with a fat ass. If it's her sister...*so be it*."

"Man, you make it sound like it ain't shit but bro, that's her *sister,* dawg!" I thought about it out loud as he spoke.

"Even still...that's not on *you* to be more loyal to *Sister A* than her *sister* is," he opined. "If she asks about it, you tell her. Otherwise, you just move how you move under the assumption that *Sister B* ain't hiding shit from *Sister A*."

He's saying nearly the same shit the ~~beast~~ does but hearing it from Ricky made it make more sense to me. I may just be overthinking all this shit. And it's not like Shonne told me *not* to say anything to Lisa. It's *gotta* be full disclosure between them. I ain't that important to risk falling out with your sibling over...*right?* No dick is that good.

After my conversation with Ricky, I decide that he's right. *Sister B* knows I fucked *Sister A*...and she just want the **HoLLyWooD** now that her sister done moved on. There's no harm here. Lisa told us to stop flirting but then had a conversation with her offline...and Shonne said she was grown enough to make her own decisions.

"Whatever happens after that is between them as sisters. That ain't on you, HoLLy."

107

*   *   *   *   *

Shonne and I keep chatting and texting for a few more weeks. Our conversations get intense.

It's wild how her and her sister compare to each other. Shonne also is bisexual and a huge nymph. She's got an appetite for sex that isn't easily satisfied, and she has to cum multiple times in one day. Her dude – he doesn't fuck her as long as she needs or as often as she wants it. It's crazy how many times I've heard that a nigga can't keep up with these freaks out here.

She tells me about her *PornHub* obsession, how she watches my *Twitter* timeline daily for all the retweets of ass and titties. It helps her through her horniness at work. She ain't shy, either, which I could tell from her flirty nature. But she ain't got no butterflies in her stomach or cold feet when it comes to her body – she loves to show it off. She's proud of her shape after 2 kids...and she sends me a *lot* of nudes. She's in love with her own ass...she knows what she working with. She's also got an oral fixation...she's gotta have something in her mouth often. Of course, y'all know where the conversations go with that. And she ain't no punk about it at all. She tells me she's gon suck my dick over and over without her jaws getting tired.

Cooking is a real obsession for Shonne. We spend a lot of our talks about food. She tells me when she gets in town, she's gonna go grocery shopping at the store across from my building and cook enough food for me to eat for another week. She's so excited to cook. She wants to see all the food places that St. Louis has to offer, too…the girl is super stoked about going to *Sweetie Pies*. And she also wants to try the chicken at the infamous strip club, *Bottoms Up*. She heard them wings be fire. So, part of her agreement to visit centers around me letting her have her way about food. Fair trade. She decides to come see me the 3rd weekend of November.

It's hard not to think it could be a setup, the way it's all playing out. But shit, at this point…the plan is in motion. If it's all a trick…I guess I'ma find out soon enough.

Right?

*   *   *   *   *

12

So I'm expecting Shonne around 7:30pm on that Friday.

I had the whole day to myself and I decided to check out a movie that afternoon...alone. I was nearly a full-blown loner in St. Louis, so going to the movies solo had become a thing for me. The original plan that day was to see a movie with Sug, but me and that bitch had been through so much since moving here that we could barely stand to be in the same room some days. This day was one of those days, and I ended up at the show alone after another pointless fight.

"Sometimes I wish I never met that bitch..."

It may have been a good thing we fell out though, so Sug wasn't checking for me over the weekend. I kept a low profile in the Lou – so if I was spotted out with Shonne, there was very little chance it would get back. But then again, if Sug and I were into it, she prolly would almost *expect* me to be with another bitch. Prefer it, even.

Anyway, the movie ends around 5:40pm and that gives me a little time to get ready for the outta-town pussy. I hurry home to my downtown loft...one that I call

The Layher.

I name all my spots…it's another *HoLLy* form of expression. After Shay left and I moved to the downtown apartment near *Lookout Point* back in KC, I called that place *The Boom Boom Room*…for being like my permanent hotel suite that was ever necessary to get over *Sashé.*

And then after that…there was the ever-legendary *Graham Suites* loft. Aaaaaaah…the *Graham Suites*. The loft overlooking *Kansas City Power & Light District*. That's where my belligerence really started to take flight.

Lisa knew all about the *Graham Suites*…I moved there from the *Boom Boom Room* a week after I finally tapped that. That's where I *really* put it on her…I mean put it down *for real*. I thought I was *HoLLyRod Hefner* up in the *Graham Suites* – the memories are crazy.

But now, I was in *The Layher*, a smaller, open space studio style loft in downtown Saint Louis. This was supposed to be my follow-up to the *Graham Suites*, and a getaway from *Sug*. There was a bar separating the kitchen and living room…and a sliding wall next to the bathroom that sectioned off the bedroom from the living room.

I straighten up my place a bit, and once everything is in order, I sit down to vape some *GG* before my company arrives. Shonne calls me at like 7:15 and I guide her to my street from the highway before meeting her outside.

112

Ok, so now I'm finally seeing her for the first time in person. And it isn't until now that this hits me – I'm meeting somebody off *Twitter*. I mean, it isn't the first time I've met someone off *Twitter*...or the internet for that matter. But I'm tripping as she's getting out the car, because after all – I used to fuck the dog shit outta her sister not long ago. And until about five weeks ago, I didn't even know she existed. This brings me back to my thoughts on the *social media matrix*....and I realize again that as times continue to change, I've continued to stay evolving since day one.

"This is how you know the Curse is real..."

I've probably talked to this girl on the phone three times...mostly texting and pic messages. Yet she's found a babysitter, hopped in her bucket, and drove over 300 miles to spend the weekend with me.

Did I agree to pay for gas? For some reason...I can't remember if I did. I hope so. For the purposes of telling this story, let's just say *I did*...so I don't feel like such an ass.

So, I'm at her door, helping her out the car. Shonne is shorter than Lisa...maybe 5'1". As she puts her arms around my neck and we share our first hug, the bulge in my pants pokes her left thigh, "Damn, ok HoLLy. Can I get out the car first?!"

"My bad," I apologized unapologetically. "Where ya bags at?"

She's got two bags in the back seat. I tell her I got 'em…it bothers me to see a female carrying bags n'shit like that, so I'm just being me. Don't ask me to make it make sense.

There's a long hallway in my lobby and the elevators are to the right down a second hallway. I tell her to walk ahead of me…and it's like a déjà vü. I'm behind her, watching her ass flex as she walks. Lisa had a mean walk. Shonne is just as thick, with a switch just as synchronized.

HOW THE FUCK DO THEY PULL THIS SHIT OFF?!?!?!

My dick is jumping in my pants…and this time, I don't try to play it off.

We get to the 6th floor…and I tell her to take a left down the hall to get to my loft at the opposite end. She's talking to me about the drive, how it took forever and how she can't wait to relax. But first, she wants to go across the street to the *Culinaria* and get groceries. She doesn't want me to go, but I insist. I mean, *who's gonna carry the bags?* Right.

Shonne is soaking all this up. She can't believe I'm single, no kids, and this much of a gentleman wrapped up in an asshole's body. If she only knew.

She's extra touchy-feely and affectionate…a slight difference from Lisa. Lisa was touchy-feely…but only

114

once we were naked. Shonne is all over me, though. In the elevator, out the front door, on the way across the street to the store. She smells good...I can't make out the fragrance, but it's a powder-fresh type scent. I'm cuffing her ass in her brown capri pants...thinking about how wrong it is to show favoritism amongst siblings.

When we get to the checkout line...Shonne's phone rings, and she's still talking to me as she pulls it out her purse, "So do you want lasagna or chicken alfredo? I just got a taste for some pasta! Oh...hold on, this is my sister calling..."

Aww damn. Here we go. The moment of truth...

"Hello?" she answered. "Girl, nothing...at this grocery store. Yep. I'm in St. Louis. I made it about an hour ago."

*   *   *   *   *

13

Wow...so *Shonne* is talking to *Lisa*, telling her how she made it to St. Louis.

"Ok, there's your confirmation, HoLLy. Can you let it go now?"

Lisa *has* to know, Shonne ain't hiding nothing...she *can't* be. She's telling her how she's gonna be here 'til Sunday and how she gotta go to *Sweetie Pies* before she leaves. They on the phone laughing, I mean this shit is fucking me up low-key. Ever the smooth one, I don't let it show. Never let 'em see you sweat. I keep my cool and play bag-boy, waiting 'til we get back to my loft before asking Shonne about Lisa, "Damn, so Lisa know wassup, huh?"

"What you mean, baby?" Shonne asked in a confused tone.

"Wit you fucking with me..."

She's putting some of the food in my refrigerator and spreading the rest on the bar, "I mean, she knows...yea. She saw us talking on *Twitter*...and she know I'm in St. Louis. So – yea – she knows."

"I'm just saying. I haven't talked to her; we don't talk for real anymore. That's *yo* sister..."

Shonne looks off in space, in deep thought, "I mean,

117

she gotta know – right? Hell, I don't know, it's not like I'm telling her my every move. But at the same time, it's still *my business*. I told you I'm grown. That's my **little** sister, remember?"

"You sholl right," I had to agree with her. We all grown as fuck.

"I told you to let it go, nigga. What more you need to hear?"

"I got it, bro. That's the last time I'm mentioning it to her. Fuck it – I'm not in it.

Later that night, after I was good and full from the alfredo, me and Shonne sat on the couch, drinking as we watched old episodes of *The Wire*. The bitch made a bunch of food and I was full as fuck. Fixed my plate, made my drink – the whole nine. Then she cleans my entire kitchen and folds my clothes up that were sprawled across the bed.

Sister B was definitely more domesticated. It made sense. It also made my dick hard. Any man is turned on by a woman in the kitchen serving him. Shonne knew that would make an impression on me.

That *'in the kitchen, catering'* shit is a great quality to have – a necessity if you ever plan on being a wife. Ain't no point in wifing you if you can't take care of me and the kids…be a homemaker first. I dig that shit. I miss that shit. And I had that hands down with KeLLy.

I never think about her these days, but Kells had the nurturing down to a tee. Ain't no woman that knew how to take better care of a household than KeLLy. I never had to worry about cooking, cleaning, or any of that shit with her. KeLLy genuinely just loved to do it. She said that's how she was raised to be as a woman. She spoiled me…and I didn't realize so many chicks out here lacked that quality in 'em. And right now, I'm reminded of that characteristic in Shonne. The way she making sure a nigga eats and how she's eager to do that type of work without me expecting it…that shit is taking me back to a time when things were more normal.

It's just too bad I'm not tryna wife this hoe. I mean, she's on the highway for dick while somebody else watch the kids. I'm impressed with Shonne…but not blown off course. I remind myself how these last two years with Sug have helped erase *any* thoughts about wifing a bitch, no matter how domesticated she is. I've got a mission to accomplish.

Shonne makes the first move…unless you count me playing with her booty the whole time we chilled. I'm on the left side on the couch, Shonne is laying her head on my right thigh, her body curled up. My right hand has been all over her ass all night.

She seems so much smaller than Lisa…but this ass…*man look*. Her ass looks even bigger in the pink boy shorts, her cuff just rounded off perfectly. I'm squeezing, reaching down near her pussy, but not touching it. My dick is laying on my left thigh and starts to get hard…right near Shonne's head.

She turns her body over to her right, and now she's on her back…looking up at me. Head still in my lap. We stare at each other, and I rub my fingers on her inner left thigh, "You good??"

Shonne lets out a half-moan, half-whisper, "Very good…"

119

"Lemme see," I grab her whole pussy through her panties with my hand...rubbing my fingers across her lips. I can feel the wetness as she squeezes her legs together, trapping my hand down there momentarily.

She moans and flips back over suddenly...grabbing my dick with her right hand, "Come on, pull it out..."

As I lift up to pull my gym shorts off...she sits up on all fours, bent over. Before my shorts hit the floor, she's got her right hand in her panties...playing with her pussy. I stand up straight ...hovering over her, lifting her t-shirt to rub her naked back. Her skin is soft as fuck. She puts her head down on the couch, moaning gently. My dick is standing straight out, lingering above her head.

Her ass is so round and meaty...I wanna bite a chunk out this muhfucka. Instead, I bend my knees slightly and grab her cheek with my right hand, and then, just as quickly, slap it with my palm roughly. Her back caves in a little, and she lifts her head up...taking my dick in her mouth to a pool of drool.

Fuuuuuuuuuuck...

My knees buckle and I almost fall into the table behind me, but I catch my balance by grabbing the back of her head and forcing myself deeper into her throat. Her jaws are stuck tight around my **wooD** as she moans...sounding sexy as fuck.

I've got her short bob in a fist, ready to guide her up and down my shaft slowly...but her pace and motion is *perrrrfect.* Her throat opens wider as she goes down deeper, then her jaws close down tightly as she comes up and just sucks the head. No hands. A large ball of spit falls from her mouth to the couch...and I move in closer, causing her to fall backwards...

"Damn, you nasty," I mumbled lowly.

She takes my dick in her hand...stroking it with her saliva, "I know. Sit down."

She sits up on her knees and I sit back on the couch. She never stops jacking my dick until my butt hits the pillows. I pull my wife-beater over my head and toss it across the room, and it falls to the wooden floor next to the bathroom doorway.

"Lay back, HoLLy," she instructed with confidence.

I oblige...taking her ass cheek in hand again and lifting her towards me. Her head falls back in my lap and my dick jumps up, hitting the side of her face. And she swallows it again with the swiftness. Sucking and tugging at it with her lips...a slimy film of spit making it shiny under my ceiling spotlights. I start pulling her hair with lustful aggression, "Hell yea...suck that shit. *Slooow.* Just like that. Daaaamn. *Damn Shonne...*"

The voice of my beast must motivate her because she speeds up her bobbing. But only by a bit. I take my right hand in my own mouth...drooling on my fingers. Then, I reach under her panties and in her ass crack...rubbing her tight hole. She starts sucking me even sloppier...

I can feel the buildup in my nuts...and I pull my legs apart, humping at her mouth. She's taking every thrust in stride as my beast starts to take over, "*Fuuuck,* you so fuckin nasty girl! Hell...fuuuckin...*right.* You suckin' that muhfuckin' dick. *Keep sucking that shit like.... fuuuuck girl!* You gon let me cum in ya mouth? *Huh bitch?* You...you hear me?? You gon lemme cum in ya mouth Shonne...???"

*   *   *   *   *

14

For maybe a half a second, I have an outta-body experience and trip off what's happening.

I've really got my dick in this chick's mouth....and I fucked her sister not long ago. If it was a trick to this shit...I missed it.

"I told you, nigga! Sibling rivalry!"

She's gagging on it now, fucking her throat voluntarily...rubbing her own clit and squirming on the couch. This whole scene is making me red with adrenaline, and before Shonne can give me permission...it's too late.

I bite my lip as I release in her mouth...dick throbbing repeatedly while I shoot gulps down her throat. She doesn't flinch or stop at all...making slurpy sounds, forcibly gripping with her hands to help drain me. My balls are soaked, as the spit runs down my shaft and onto the couch. She's still sucking...and I'm trying to push her away.

It's not working. She's sucking me off with a newfound fury now...pushing me against the pillows, hand firmly on my chest.

125

"*You nasty...lit...little....*" I stuttered in the voice of my *beast*.

I wasn't prepared for this...my hairs are standing up on the back of my neck. I look over to my right at her ass in the air – I didn't even see her come out her panties. But sure enough, she's got her bare ass up in the air now. I start grabbing and scratching it, a strong rush of aggression running through me. I've gotta fuck this chick, like right now.

I push her away, this time grabbing her shoulder with returned firmness, "*I'm 'bout to fuck the shit outta you...*"

I stand up and tell her to get naked. All she had left was her shirt and bra...those dropped quickly. I tell her to walk to the room, and I follow behind her...jacking my dick off slowly, which is still dripping with her mouth juice. Her pussy is leaking down her legs as she walks.

Why is this so arousing to me?

She walks in my bedroom area and hops up on the bed, ass in the air. She knows exactly how she wants to take this dick...and that's just how I give it to her. Sliding in Shonne's creamy pussy for the first time felt like a wet dream. My dick was so hard, she didn't even notice how I busted another nut almost instantly...

*   *   *   *   *

We go at it like jackrabbits all night. Shonne wasn't lying when she said she had an oral fixation...this bitch kept my dick in her mouth most of the night. She even slept with her head on my stomach so she could wake up and put her mouth on it. She must have done that three or four times before we finally crawled outta bed the next day, sometime after 2pm. Well, I'd be more accurate to say that she gotta outta bed. I had drunk nearly a fifth of *Henn* by myself the night before...so I stayed in bed while she took a shower.

So now I have a moment to myself to consider what just happened. I should feel bad right? I don't. I actually can't wait to tell **Ricky** and **Jaz** that I pulled this shit off. Ricky – he won't be surprised after all the shit we've been on with the hoes over the years. But Jaz...this nigga is gonna be floored – as floored as he was when I told him this actually *was* Lisa's blood sister. I know it's immature to have these thoughts fresh out the pussy...but I mean come on, if you were me, you wouldn't?

I *am* starting to believe that Shonne is doing this behind Lisa's back for some reason, though I can't figure why. Again, I don't know their relationship, but *something* seems a little off. I just couldn't put my finger on it. Oh well...like I decided before...I'm not in it. I just wanna relish in my accomplishment for a little bit, and not worry about the drama that may come later.

Later that night, me and Shonne hit up the strip club. This is where the shit gets lit. We're already drunk when we head out. She likes *Patron* and has been taking shots for the last hour. She was feeling some type of way most of the night, sucking me up twice before we got dressed.

I'm wearing blue jeans and a brown and white striped Polo button down, and Shonne has on a black one-piece short romper hugging her cheeks tight. I wanna fuck this bitch in the elevator on the way downstairs. Once we get to *My Precious*, she starts complaining about her panties…saying she shoulda bought an extra thong.

"Damn, you that wet already?" I was surprisingly shocked.

"No, but I will be later," Shonne smirked. "I shoulda thought about it."

"You wanna go back to the loft?" I asked, re-opening my door.

"No, I don't feel like doing all'at," she stopped me. "Put some porn on…come on."

"What you wanna watch?" I reached in the back seat and picked up the DVDs. There's only three of them, and they all X-rated.

"*Hot Black MILFS???*" Shonne laughed. "Put this one in."

So we're leaving the garage, there's porn playing in the dashboard of the Lac...and we're headed across the water to the East Side. I have no idea what type of night to expect...other than I know I'm getting some pussy later. It's been a minute since I went to the strip clubs. I been tryna stay outta them muhfuckaz after all the shit me and Sug been into – and again that's another story.

But this Shonne chick is a different type of freak...I know she bout to be on one once we hit the club. See, Lisa had a little bit of innocence left, just a *little* bit of reserve. The big sister is a lot more open about hers...and more *seasoned*....at least at this point. Remember I said that.

"Ooooo, are we gon find a bitch to take home??? Please say yeah, HoLLy."

*　　　*　　　*　　　*　　　*

We get back from the club around 4:45am...just the two of us. I'm tired from clubbing all night. We went to three different spots...trying to find a girl that Shonne liked. We had no luck. But I did grab a bunch of tits and ass...sampling the goods with Shonne on some auction shit.

I learned while in love with Shay how ***ménages*** are

129

always easier said than done. So, in the end, we didn't find anybody Shonne deemed as worthy, and we called it a night before the sun started to come up. But without even making it clear, neither one of us planned on any sleep.

We hit the bedroom, hands all over each other. Kissing and licking at each other's necks...tripping over shoes. I rip the top of her outfit, and she stops for a second to curse, then bites the side of my face. I answer with a hard smack across the top of her ass...I mean the ass pokes out so much that it's easy. She's tearing my belt off...

Both of us are ass naked...and my back crashes against the bed first. She crawls up on the mattress, head going for my dick...but I pull her upwards and motion for her to turn around, "*Put that pussy on my face, bitch!*"

I reach for her ankles, and she squats above my face. Her pussy lips are fat and completely bare...juices dripping as I catch it on my chin. She takes my whole dick in her throat as I stick my tongue straight up and lower her onto it. Her pussy muscles start gripping my tongue and her ass cheeks tighten up. She grabs my right ankle, holding on for dear life as she rides my tongue...her sweet wetness splashing all over my face.

The 69 goes on for about nine minutes straight. I cum and she keeps going. She drenches my face with her orgasm...and I grab her by the waist to hold her in place. No favoritism.

She's still slurping up and down on my **wooD**...and

it feels like I'm gonna cum again. But I wanna fuck…so I push her off my face, lift up and toss her to the side…trying to get to a condom before I bust again. It doesn't work. I can feel cum dripping and oozing out my shit…all over the sheets and her back while I walk across the bed in haste. I hop down to the wooden floor and reach under my mattress. Shonne is bent over, looking me in the eye.

"*Turn yo ass around…*" I said in the voice of my *beast*.

Shonne obeys without saying anything, taking the sheets in both her hands and bracing herself. Her ass looks lovely in the moonlight glaring through my blinds. I give it three nice and hard slaps before I shove my dick in, still standing up on the floor. I start ramming her from behind; my dick is hard as brick. She's pulling the sheets off the mattress, cursing loudly. I'm in full *beast-mode* now.

"*You like this dick, don't you…you like how I'm fucking you Shonne? You nasty little freak…I can't hear you!!!*"

I slap her ass again and pull out, taking a couple steps back. She's begging me to put it back in. I push her forward, so hard her head bumps the wall. I act like I ain't see it, climbing onto the bed behind her.

She's still bent over…and now I'm squatting. Hands on her waist…and pounding away deep in her pussy. I can feel her cervix…her muscles are tightening up. It's splashing. If I ain't know no better…I'd think she was about to squirt.

I lean over her, pull her closer so I can play with Sister B's round B-cups. Her nipples are hard and long, but perfectly proportioned with her perky bust. She starts throwing it back, as much as she can with my tight grip around her body.

We fuck until about 6:30 in the morning before falling asleep. I wake up after a couple of hours, with her sprawled all over me...and I start licking her pussy again, waking her up. She tells me to be gentle because it's sore. Once I hear those words...I get up to get a condom...and beat some more redness into her until I came again, crashing down on top of her.

We finally get up around 1 o'clock to get *Sweetie Pies* before I send her on her way back down I-70.

So Big Booty Shonne ends up being a good piece of ass – right? On my next couple of trips to KC, we get it in and she cooks breakfast afterwards. We don't develop any relationship other than purely sexual...and every time we fuck – she feeds me, so it's a win. For a while, *Sister B* becomes the perfect distraction from my train wreck with Sug, and the rough year ends on a better note.

As I shoulda expected though, over the next few months I would soon be reminded that nothing lasts forever without drama.

Especially when it comes to mingling with family in this thing called the *Art of Cheating*...

*   *   *   *   *

One more time before I continue, it's important to talk about the year I had leading up to meeting Shonne. Bear with me…

2011 had been full of humbling and life-altering moments. But perhaps the biggest event that stood out was my hasty breakup with the music.

My affair with music had started right before my affair with Shay. It's no secret that deep down I felt like when I left Kells for Shay, I was also leaving KeLLy for the music. Music became my life after that, and the wild habits with Shay kept me inspired musically. But you know the story by now. Shay then bounced on me and left me feeling unmotivated. It took a while for the melodies to fill my head again, but I found a way to temporarily keep going by feeding off the energy of my beast.

The rampage that followed had led to me somehow falling for Suga B. I know now that it was the music that made it possible. If I wasn't at the studio working on my project that day we met…well, I mean, we woulda never crossed paths. If it wasn't for Sug's musical talent and willingness to work on ideas with me…we woulda never started getting as close. That's likely why I was so blindsided in becoming so attached to Sug at a time where I was trying to remain technically single. I was focusing so much on not falling for girls like Lisa, I ain't have my guard up for where the music was taking me with Sug.

The music had become my gateway to new levels of

133

toxic boldness and a new world of belligerence with Sug. But eventually, my focus became less about the music and more about the tangled web we were weaving. My beast continued to get greedier. The deeper my relationship with Sug got, the harder everything became to juggle.

Then Sug and I started to fall apart heading into 2011, and everything else in my world also started to crumble. Back-to-back deaths in the family. I had a long streak of writer's block with the music. The drinking and the drugs increased. I stopped going to therapy with Dr. Julie. The first few months of the year were crazy, and it broke me down. I needed something to point the finger at.

I started to suddenly believe my string of misfortune might be related to me misreading the energy of the Curse. What if all this crazy shit was happening because I was never supposed to chase the music in the first place? Sug was my 3rd relationship in the last 5 years to fall apart during my music journey. Look at how it had made my inner beast even more of a monster over the years. What if I really *was* supposed to steer clear away from the stage after all…like my Pops and Grandpa Jerry before me?

These second thoughts influenced me to walk away from my music career abruptly in the spring of 2011, much to the dismay of many in my circle, especially Jaz and Ricky Rhymes. One day I'd had enough and just gave it all up, cancelling my already-delayed album release without another thought.

It only felt like the right decision for a few days.

Things got progressively worse, and after falling out with
my camp over calling it quits, I started distancing myself
from the world in general. Sug and I kept fighting. The
depression and anxiety increased. I was going through it
and starting to believe I'd never be understood by those
closest to me. Hell, I barely could understand myself
anymore. I had fallen completely off. How did I go
through all'at shit to get my lick back with Sashé...only to
end up in an even worse position of vulnerability with
Sug?

Was it the music I shoulda left alone or was it Sug?
Did I get it wrong again? The pace to rock bottom sped
up after I killed the music – there was no denying that.
Still, it had been nearly impossible to start blaming my
decisions with Sug. Sure, I always knew the life we got
involved in was wrong, but I was in too deep and couldn't
see myself without her. I didn't wanna let her go, but the
beast was determined to change that. By that summer, it
felt like deja vü, like my recovery situation with Shay all
over again.

2011 ended for me in contrast to how it had started
though, and by the time Big Booty Shonne fell in my lap, I
had started to regain some mental strength and energy.
Shortly afterwards, Sug and I had another big fight and
she was ready to call it quits for real this time. But I had
new pussy around again, so this time...for the first
time...I didn't try to stop her from leaving. Don't get me
wrong...I was still hooked on Sug, so allowing her to walk
away wuttin' no easy task. I couldn't have done it without
that voice in my head, promising me it was for the best.

Once the end of December hit, I had decided to give the artistry another shot and get back to being myself again. The music was calling me back. My writer's block had disappeared, and the bars were flowing again. Pops always told me I could never escape my fate. Isolating myself had given me more clarity...shit didn't seem so cloudy anymore by the end of 2011.

The last year and a half had been a real eye-opener for a nigga...and it felt like I had finally figured out the lessons the universe had been trying to teach me through all of the hardship. I'd left Sug alone. For the first time ever – it was just me and my inner conflicts. No main chick, no side chicks. No roster full of bitches to keep me on my toes in *The Art*. It was a good feeling to truly have a fresh start and it was a long time coming.

February 2012

So I'm in Kansas City on a cold winter night recording at Jaz's. I decide I wanna fuck Shonne when I'm done working for the night. Big Booty Shonne was pretty much the only chick I was fucking consistently by now and we had a good thing.

Until we didn't...

When she picked up the phone that night...she started talking like I never heard before.

"Wassup...I'm 'bout to be on my way over there," I

told her. I could immediately tell that something was off, though.

"Maaaaan. I don't know, HoLLy," Shonne sounded unsure.

"You don't know what?" I asked, irritated.

"Cuuuuz man. I been feeling kinda bad lately."

"What the fuck you even talmbout right now?" I snapped. "Feeling bad about what?"

"Cuuuz…I can't be doing my sister like that," she confessed.

"Yo sister?!?!" I yelled. "*Lisa???* Huh? Why we talking about her? I thought she knew about us!"

*   *   *   *   *

15

Shonne tried to calm me down, "She does know. Well, I mean, *I don't know*. We ain't never really talk about it…"

"I mean…what is you saying???" I shook my head. I wuttin' tryna hear this bullshit right about now.

"I'm saying I just assumed she *knew* what was up, but I don't know now. She made a comment to our other sister about it. So, I don't know. I just don't wanna keep feeling guilty about this shit, HoLLy," she pleaded.

Now all of a sudden this muhfucka got a guilty conscience?? I been fucking Shonne every now and then for almost three months now. Why is she bringing up her sister?

I hadn't talked to *Lisa* often at all since I started fucking Shonne. There was this weekend last month when we linked up, but…it wuttin' like that.

Lisa was in the Lou in January for a photoshoot. She called me to kick it; to take her and her friend to the strip club. *Ok, that part is ironic, I know. But still.* All we did was kicked it.

I mean, lemme be clear. We got high, we got fucked up, and they spent the night at *The Layher*. We slept in the same bed, so of course, I tried to play with that pussy. I mean, that woulda been a real epic twist to the story – right? But Lisa wuttin' having it, so what does it matter? She stopped me when my hands got close, like the very first time we laid together.

The point is – by January, I had been fucking Lisa's sister for a couple of months now and she *must* have known at that point, right? Why else would she stop me from fucking? Because now that I'm fucking Sister B…Sister A can't gimme no more pussy. Right?

Well, on the other hand, it *coulda* been that Lisa was tryna be faithful to her guy, I suppose. Lisa had turned into somewhat a good girl by 2012. Somewhat anyway.

Whatever the case was, we hadn't talked since that night a month ago. And there was no bad blood between me and Lisa. So in my mind, again, I'm assuming Lisa knew about Shonne and was ok with it. As crazy as it sounds, I had just been moving like that was the case.

I can't say I was ever convinced that Shonne was completely open with her about it though. I always felt like that, but again, I also can't say why a *sister* would be on that kind of shit. So I've always ignored that gut feeling.

Now that Shonne is talking with all this doubt about our situation…it's all coming back.

"I mean, I just don't see how you feel guilty now, after all this time," I wondered. "We already fucked, more than twice. What difference do it make now? Quit playing!"

"I'm not!" Shonne shot back. "I just don't think it's

right. And I don't want that bad karma…"

She's starting to piss me off, and I've had more than a few drinks, "Man see, you on dat bullshit. That's a cop out! You ain't gotta be on that fake shit with me! Keep it a hunnid…"

"Boy boo! I am! Ain't nobody being fake!"

I wasn't convinced, "Sound like you just tryna get some other dick to me. Which is cool if that's the case, but just say that though. You talked all'at shit when I was on the highway…how you been horny n'shit! Now I'm tryna come through, and you on some saint shit??"

She smacked her lips, "First of all, I ain't had no other dick in hellas!! And then, I mean, damn, Rodney! That's my sister!!"

"She was yo sister long before I met you….so whatever!" I shot back. "You on some bull!!!"

"So, you mad at me now??" she asked softly.

"I ain't mad. I'm cool," I shrugged.

"Yeah, you are…I can hear it in ya voice, HoLLy…"

"Look, I said I ain't mad," I bit my lip. "I'll just talk to you later."

So, I hang up with Shonne, not mad…but in a horny rage. Frustrated and needing to let off some steam – I end up calling one of my old down bitches in KC…***Carmen***.

Carmen was part of the reason Sug and I fell out last

year, and we hadn't talked in months. As a matter of fact, it had reached the point where I promised Sug that I would cut Carmen off in an attempt to fix us. But now Sug was no longer around...and Shonne had pissed me and the ~~beast~~ off.

If it's one thing I can't stand, it's an unstable bitch. Carmen took real good care of me that night, and the minute that Shonne got on some inconsistent shit with me...she lost my interest.

The next few trips to KC...Shonne doesn't get a call from HoLLy. But calling Carmen and reopening up our energy that night was beyond pivotal. Remember I said that.

*　　*　　*　　*　　*

March 2012

Ok, so dig this. I'm drunk and on *Twitter*...talking shit about how cold my head game is. I mean, 'cause it is...that's no secret. Carmen starts making comments, so now we're talking shit back and forth. Then outta nowhere, *Shonne,* of all people, gets on and chimes in.

Of course, the **DM's** soon follow.

Shonne tells me we should fuck one last time...for old time's sake. I ask her about her guilt trip...and she's

142

like she ain't feeling that shit no more and now she needs that **HoLLyDick**☐. I'm hesitant…but I like having my ego stroked, so I tell her to keep talking. Then she says…she wants to have a *ménage*.

With *Carmen*.

Ok…I'm strong. But not that strong. I've had this fantasy fulfilled plenty of times at this point…but not nearly ever enough. *Ménages* will always be my weakness.

Keep talking, Big Booty Shonne….

Shonne says she's serious. She tells me that I should see if Carmen is with it and next time I'm in town, we need to all get down.

Ok. I'm not that fucking strong!!!!!!

By the next day, I've got Carmen texting Shonne and vice versa. Straight **HoLLyBeLLigerence** – right? I'm still out for blood. I mean…I ain't really convinced that I wanna go through with it – but it seems like Shonne is always trying to take shit the extra mile. And the way my ~~beast~~ is set up – I ain't never the one who ain't gon see how far you willing to go.

But I really don't trust this bitch. It's something she not telling me. I don't know man, I just got this gut feeling that she got some motive, some untold truth that she hiding in front of.

So, I start asking around. And here's what I end up finding out:

Shonne's been fucking the same guy that her younger sister Lisa is chasing forever with.

Ok, I ain't no hater. And the *cheat gawds* know I been on a belligerent routine the last couple of years. But I'm also not in it for the *drama*. So, without warning, I cut off contact with Shonne once I found this out. This bitch was starting to turn into the evil older sister with a jealous streak or something. Like damn…she on some real hoe shit. Right?

Whatever she on…I ain't signed up for it. And the pussy is good…it's nice and wet. Her throat game was pretty spectacular. But is it worth this type of energy? Lisa's cat was tighter and her ass was bigger. So, it's not like I woulda be giving up the better prize by cutting this hoe off. I just ain't want nothing else to do with her at this point.

Well after about a week and a half, Shonne decides to confront me via text about the sudden lack of contact or replies.

SHONNE: "So why you acting funny with me for real? Wassup??"

ME: "I'm not acting funny, I'm just good…"

144

SHONNE: "Obviously not, I mean you don't even talk to me and when you do you say evil or smart shit. Something is up."

ME: "I'm good Shonne..."

SHONNE: "..."

SHONNE: "Dude what is it? Tell me what u in ya feelings about."

ME: "Girl ain't nobody in no feelings, I told u I'm good. You too messy."

SHONNE: "Messy? How am I messy? What are you even talking about?"

ME: "I don't trust you. You a liar and u messy. I'm good on u."

SHONNE: "What I lie to you about?"

ME: "You said u wasn't getting no other dick. That's a lie."

SHONNE: "Omg...what?!?! We not together...I didn't know I was supposed to tell you if or who I'm fucking! whereDeyDoDatAt ?"

ME: "You right, we not together. That's why u didn't have to lie to me about that. And then it's messy for you to be fuckin WHO you been fuckin..."

SHONNE: "Messy how?"

ME: "Cuz it seems like you got an obsession playing with Lisa's toys..."

SHONNE: "Oh wooooow!!!! Are u serious? Omg! Well it's not my fault Lisa got so many toys..."

"Wow this bitch is a savage," even my ~~beast~~ thinks she's wild for this.

SHONNE: "That's what u tripping off of???

ME: "I'm not tripping. I just said I'm good."

SHONNE: "So you not gon gimme dat??"

ME: "Bye Shonne."

SHONNE: "Whatever HoLLy!!!"

That's the last time I hear from Shonne for a few more weeks.

*   *   *   *   *

Late March 2012

I'm clowning on Twitter again – right? This time I'm tweeting about taking applications for a baby mama, on some real Grandpa Jerry shit. I get a few responses and shit-talking, but one in *particular* catches my attention.

@LusciousLisaaa: "@HoLLyAintShit I told you before we'd have some cute babies lmbo!"

Aww, how cute. Lisa ain't been on Twitter in a minute.

Nigga, I know you miss that booty! I sure the fuck do...

See, now here you go! I'm not doing the Drummer Boy Jerry nigga...I don't care how good Lisa's pussy is!

Just let it play out, HoLLy...

@HoLLyAintShit: "@LusciousLisaaa stop playing, u was supposed to been got preggo lol"

@LusciousLisaaa: "@HoLLyAintShit I'm readdddy!!!"

So, we have this little cute exchange in the Matrix and get a nice laugh out of it – the both of us only half-serious. Like I said before, it ain't never been no bad blood with Lisa.

Well then later that day, *Shonne* hops in my texts.

SHONNE: "So we going out for drinks when you come to town?"

ME: "Lol no..."

SHONNE: "Why? You can bring ya future bm too, it'll be fun."

$$* \qquad * \qquad * \qquad * \qquad *$$

S1E3: HoLLy BeLLigerence

16

"Oh, so now this bitch wanna be funny???"

"Calm down, HoLLyRod," my beast tries to tell *me* to chill for a change.

"Nah man, fuck that! She got the wrong one, nigga! She wanna be on some belligerent shit? Bet."

It's only one way I know how to kill this energy with Shonne. So, I send a text of my own out:

ME: "Hey stranger...what you up to?"

LISA: "Nothing much. How u been future bd? ;)"

ME: "I been good, Lisa boo. doing my thing."

LISA: "That's good. Yeah I been trying to do my own thing too. Getting rid of fake people in my life..."

Hmm. What have we here? What's this about?

ME: "Yeah I feel that, me too. Don't get rid of me tho! Again, I mean lol..."

LISA: "Lol HoLLy u ain't never been fake wit me. Wish I could say the same about so-called loved ones tho."

ME: "I'm nosy. What happened?"

LISA: "I'm not trying to bore you with my drama lol. I just had to see some people for who they really are. Lesson learned."

ME: "Lol I mean who u talmbout...ya hubby? What – u caught him cheating or something?"

LISA: "LMBO! You would be the one to say that! No. But I'm single now. Niggas ain't shit!!!"

ME: "This is true. But you knew that already Lisa boo. I taught u at least that much..."

LISA: "LOL ok I wasn't talmbout you though! I know you ain't shit. But at least u honest about it..."

ME: "Only honest to those who I'm not dishonest with..."

LISA: "Good point. Well what about you? Are you still with Sug?

ME: "Nah. That shit ain't work out."

LISA: "Yikes! Now that's crazy right there."

ME: "How so? I mean, you know the shit we was on out here."

LISA: "Yeah but I mean – damn HoLLy! What's that – two different bitches you done broke up now with since I met you?"

ME: "Don't put it like that girl. I know I be on my bullshit...but you know I was all in with Sug. It just wasn't meant to be, ya know?"

LISA: "Yeah I feel that, that's real. I don't know why that girl had beef with me tho!! Lol what was you saying to her about me behind my back?"

ME: "Stop playing Lisa. You know I ain't never talked no shit about you behind your back. We better than that."

LISA: "Ok, yeah u right. I can honestly say that you ain't never been on no snake shit wit *me..."*

"If she only knew," the beast taunts.

"Dammit man. She can't possibly know about Shonne. Not if she talking like this. I should come clean."

"Don't do it, HoLLy. Let it go..."

"Man, fuck that. If Shonne been sneak-fucking niggas like that, Lisa doesn't know."

"So what?? Why does she need to know? Why you always making exceptions for this one, HoLLy?"

"I don't know, nigga. I'll figure it out later," I decide.

ME: "Who snaked you Lisa? I wanna know...."

LISA: "Ughhhh!!! Rodney why you always so persuasive wit me???"

ME: "Cuz you wanna be persuaded lol..."

LISA: "LOL!"

She pauses for a second before coming clean.

LISA: "Ok so, u know I been into it with my sister Shonne. She's a fuckin fake, snake bitch!"

"Uh oh…here we go."

"Let it go, HoLLy!!!"

"Nope."

ME: "What did big sis do Lisa?"

LISA: "Man what didn't she do?! First of all, I found out she been fuckin my ex. And then the bitch tried to lie about it when I confronted her. His ass tried to lie too but I expect that from a lame ass nigga for real. I'm tripping off how this bitch supposed to be my sister."

ME: "Ya ex tho? I mean…how you know it's true?"

LISA: "Because my other sister told me after her and Shonne got into it over Shonne fucking one of her ex's!!"

"Oh, damn this is the second time one of them mentioned a third sibling," I say to myself. "There's another sister?"

"Like...a Sister C?"

"This shit is getting crazy, bro."

"I told you to let it go!"

ME: "Whoa whoa whoa...wtf! Shonne fucked your other sister's ex too?? That's crazy! Ok...but still...how do you know it's all true??"

Lisa doesn't explain to me how she knows in a text. Instead, she sends me three screenshots of a text thread between Shonne and their apparent younger sister, **Mika**.

Mika and Shonne are apparently fighting about something; I didn't get the details about that part. Well anyway, Mika threatens to tell Lisa about how Shonne been fuckin her ex and Shonne is talking shit like she 'don't give a fuck'. She makes a comment like 'so what? She not gonna believe u anyway, as much as u lie!' Then Shonne threatens Mika and tells her she's got dirt on her too. Mika takes screenshots during the convo and forwards them to Lisa, and now Lisa is pissed, showing them to me.

ME: "Oh wow. Speechless."

LISA: "Ikr. And what make it so bad, Mika is sending me these screenshots and then Shonne tries to text me while they arguing on some bullshit, acting like she just 'seeing what I'm up to'. She don't know Mika sent me this shit."

ME: "Damn that's craaaaazzzzy. So, what you gonna do?"

LISA: "Hell Idk. I'm just done! I ain't got time for fake people in my life! I mean, I know my sister is a hoe – she be on hoe shit."

ME: "Yea, I can agree with that..."

LISA: "LOL u can agree??? Well damn, how you know my sister a hoe?? Did you fuck my sister too Rodney????"

ME: "Uhm...."

LISA: "Uhm? Nigga! Yes or no?"

"Let it go, HoLLy!!"

"We tell no lies in the Art, though. Remember?" I remind the ~~beast~~ sarcastically.

"Right! Half-truths though, Rod! Half-fucking-truths!!!"

"It's Lisa though, bro! I can't bullshit her."

ME: "Yeah I did. I fucked Shonne."

157

LISA: "LMAO!!! See, niggaz ain't shit!!! I shoulda knew!!!"

ME: "Lol don't say it like that. I mean..."

LISA: "Smh so when was this?? Back when y'all was flirting on Twitter and shit???"

ME: "Yeah. I fucked a few times after that. But I thought u knew, she made it out like y'all talked about me."

LISA: "Yeah we did talk about you and I told that bitch not to do it. But I should've known she would anyway. Smmfh @ u tho!"

ME: "Why??? Don't act like that!! I wasn't on no snake shit. You know I was just being belligerent. It just kind of happened."

LISA: "LOL but nigga, that's my sister!!! Why you just now telling me?"

ME: "You just now asking. We ain't been talking Lisa boo. You was caked up"

LISA: "U sholl right. Smh. That bitch got jealousy and evil in her veins! She done fucked one of Mika's niggas and two of my niggas?? Ugh!!! So, you gonna tell me how it happened HoLLy??"

ME: "What u mean? You want details?"

LISA: "Yes nigga! I'm asking, I wanna know."

ME: "Ok. Fuck it..."

"That's too belligerent, HoLLy!!"

"You telling me what's going too far now?" I couldn't believe the irony of my beast.

I didn't pull any punches. I told Lisa all about how I fucked her sister and how I had her sending nudes and cooking for a nigga. How she was driving down to get the dick and slurping me often. I mean, it's not like I wouldn't have told her before...right? We just wasn't talking. And I know I got closer to Lisa than I planned on, but what type of fling did we really have for me to look at *anyone* as off-limits? Right?

Sister or not – I was just being a nigga, much like her ex. So why get mad at the niggas being niggas? Lisa agrees somewhat. Though she feels like in the case of her ex, they actually had some serious *emotions* involved in it.

Ok fine. Well, that don't apply to HoLLy.

I fucked her sister, but Lisa and I were never officially together. She knows that. Our ongoing fling of years past was just that...a fling. We had a strange connection but we both know what it was between us.

That's what usually happens when rules in *The Art of Cheating* are followed. Ain't no need for no drama and a bunch of lies with the *'fling'* – it's just certain shit

159

you just gotta be straight up about. I have nothing to gain by being dishonest about fucking Lisa's sister, especially at this point.

"As a matter of fact...I have everything to gain by being honest right now."

"Don't do it, HoLLy. We done already fucked Carmen again, bro. Sug always hated Lisa – you know that nigga!"

"Man fuck Sug, nigga! Remember? I got this."

"I'm just saying nigga – this is ME talking. And I'm telling you...you playing a cold game right now, HoLLy."

"Yeah, well maybe I learned from the best," I snap back at the whispers in my head.

LISA: *"Damn so you just really telling me all this? You bold as hell Rodney..."*

ME: *"Whaaat? U asked about it. And I don't owe you no sugarcoat...you not my girl Lisa."*

LISA: *"Ok. So, what am I?"*

ME: *"What are you? Miss #6TimesADay ? U tell me..."*

LISA: *"Oh you got jokes!!! We bringing up all that old shit???"*

ME: "Are we?"

LISA: "I mean, don't tempt me with a good time. This ain't 'little young Lisa' asking about bringing up the old shit!"

ME: "Oh this is grown-up Lisa talking now? What does she say? Are we bringing up all'at old shit?"

LISA: "I mean...she would say: we could..."

ME: "Well I mean, when you put it like that. I say...we should..."

*   *   *   *   *

17

End of March 2012

We meet on a Saturday, just before midnight. It's been raining for most of the day, but now the wind blows calmly in a light drizzle. The room is quiet, except for the hum of the ventilation system near the window. We both stand there in silence for a few seconds.

This is wrong. We both know it. But if we gon do it…we might as well do it right. Choosing to meet in a hotel was step one, no one needs to ever know about this. The hotel accepts cash, so there's no trace on paper. No one even knows we both in this city at the same time. Man…this shit is so wrong.

I'm standing at the foot of the bed, staring at the tv screen. Lisa puts her purse on the end table, and then walks by me to my left…making eye contact. I stare her down and keep watching as she switches in front of me, close enough for me to smell her perfume. Gotdammit she smells so lovely. She's already stripped to a g-string, cheeks bouncing as she moves. Her walk is so fuccin' mean, just like I remember it.

"Nah, don't be looking at my ass, nigga!" she said with an attitude.

"I can't help it," I replied mischievously. It all feels like a deja vü, but I quickly shake it off as Lisa scurries into the bathroom. I start to undress, having already broken a sweat. There's a lot of heated lust in the air, setting tonight up as one for moments of clarity.

Lisa comes back in, walking slowly...and tells me to get in the bed. Her tone is snappy...commanding. I lay back and get comfortable as she waits with obvious impatience. Seconds later, she takes my **wooD** in her hand roughly, crawling up on the bed. Her back is arched high...ass in the air behind her, blocking my view of the widescreen tv completely. Before I can blink, she's kissing on the dick from the side – mouth salivating, wetting me up. I voluntarily make him jump, watching her lips wrapped on the shaft. Lisa moans, but disapprovingly, "Be still, Rodney."

She lifts her head and takes a firm grip at the base...slapping her face, getting her cheeks wet. I throw my head back and she starts to drool all over my erection...stroking me up and down, covering me with her warm spit.

I start to prepare for her to go to work. Only she doesn't. She then suddenly takes her hand and wipes it on her pussy.

"Damn. Like that?"

She crawls up straddling me...grabbing my chest. Then she leans in and kisses me deeply. My dick jumps up – slapping her naked ass. I reach around her to cuff her cheek...but she pushes my hands away and continues to kiss me. Wetting my face up...licking my neck. It's pissing my beast off, but her aggression is turning me on and her *resistance* is driving me crazy.

Lisa then hops off me, rolling over to the other side

of the king size bed…now lying on her back. She grabs her erect nipple in one hand and starts rubbing her pussy with the other, "You wanna watch me rub one out, HoLLy?"

Jacking my dick with anticipation, I groaned back, "Helll yeah…"

"I bet you do, nigga," she said bossily. "Now eat my pussy."

I turn over quickly, grabbing her legs to dive in…and she pushes me, "Nah…I wanna watch you jack off while you eat it. Stay on ya back."

"Nigga, is she serious?" the beast gets antsy.

First moment of clarity. It is in this moment that I realize how much of a Dom I'd turned into sexually with the beast in the picture. In this moment, I can finally remember when I felt his presence for the first time so strongly. I remember how it was a moment nearly identical to this after *KeLLy's Revenge* – where I had given up control in a kinky bedroom session. That night provoked something powerful in my inner spirit, that refused to be dominated. The last time I relinquished control like this, the energy of the beast became more than a whisper and broke loose. I've been here before.

"Ok, maybe it is deja vü. This is how we met," I remind the beast, who doesn't argue the revelation.

Lisa's energy though – it's so commanding right now. With my sloppy wet dick still in hand, I start scooting downwards…twisting my body sideways to meet her demand. She lifts her left leg up as I slide my head under…resting it on her inner right thigh.

165

Her pussy is in my face now. She's still rubbing her clit...her fingers are shiny wet. I try to lick one and she snatches her hand away, pushing my head down with aggression. I start jabbing her with my tongue, turning over on my left side.

"Yeah...hmmm!" she moaned loudly. "Yeah, nigga. Eat that shit..."

She's squeezing my head forcibly now. I'm seeing a new, *more experienced* side of Lisa. But it's the demanding vibes she's giving that's making my dick hard as steel. I start sucking her pussy lips, smacking at 'em one at a time.

"Hmmmm...stick ya tongue in my pussy, daddy! Come on...get nasty, HoLLyRod..."

I follow her lead, trying to stick it in as far as her tight hole will let me...curling my tongue upward the deeper I get. She's lifting her ass in the air...fucking my tongue back.

Fuck. Her balance is amazing.

She starts moving faster...then harder against my face. I'm slurping up her juices, twisting and turning my head around so her pussy hits my mouth from all angles. Then I turn my body to reach in with my left hand...and I start poking her, thumb helping me mouth fuck her properly.

Lisa was shaking, "Oh my gaw...don't stop Rodneee!! I'm 'bout to...'bout to! I'm...*fuuuuuck,* baby!! Shiiiiit...."

She's erupting now. The sensation is quite familiar,

and it doesn't take long to register what's happening in this second moment of clarity. Lisa is *squirting* on my face.

"Wait a minute! Since when is Big Booty Lisa a squirter???" the beast screams in my head, like a kid in a candy store.

"Nigga! That's what I'm saying! Oh my fuckin' GAWD!"

I've also been here before. Squirting is my weakness and part of what first hooked me on Sug. I can't explain it – it just takes sex to another level.

Lisa's faucet is so warm…streaming out of her smoothly. I hop on my knees and put my chin in it as she lets go. I'm holding her up by her ass cheeks…tongue out, still licking her wildly. She cums for about thirty seconds and then collapses in the puddle on the bed. I start to rub her clit…and she pushes my hand away. Again.

"No, don't touch me. I ain't done with you yet. Lay on yo back again…and keep jacking that pretty dick off."

I cut my eyes at her, realizing she's in complete control and has me right where she wants me. But there's something so sexy about her takeover, I reluctantly do as she says. Before I can blink twice, she turns around, puts her ass on my chest, and starts kissing my upper thigh softly.

"Daaaaamn, Lisa!" I squirmed. "Why you playing?"

"I'm not playing, boy," she replied, running her fingers up and down my legs. "Be still. And don't stop me."

"Stop you from wha…" my voice drifts as she stretched out on top of me and reached down to grab my

167

ankles.

"Don't move!" she sits up, scooting her booty down to my stomach. Her ass cheeks rippled in my face and I couldn't help but look away, feeling tortured. I have no idea what she's up to now.

My dick is jumping in my left hand as I reached around her thick thighs, struggling to keep stroking it. "Fuuuuck, man," I whispered.

Lisa grabs my right foot with both hands and starts massaging it gently, "Rodney, when is the last time you had your feet rubbed?"

I'm caught off guard now, and I flinched slightly. I'm almost sure I've never had a woman give me a foot rub. My initial thought is to stop her. But damn...the shit felt amazing.

"And I told you to be still, nigga!" she snapped, pressing firmly against my heel.

"Okaaaay," I groaned as my arms fell to the side in defeat.

Lisa scoots down further and her pussy is rubbing against my **wooD** now. She starts grinding into it, leaning forward to grab my other foot with her left hand. Her pussy is still dripping wet. "Hmmm...you got some smooth feet, too, baby," she said softly.

"I just got a pedicure," I admitted, halfway flustered. I was glad she couldn't see my face.

"I can tell," she lowered her head, kissing my left ankle. My toes curled in her face, and she gripped them tightly. "Stop moving."

"Maaan...dat shit tickle, man!" I whined.

"Nah, you been doing what the fuck you wanna do since we met. Let me have this, daddy," she demanded, licking the top of my foot slowly. "I ain't even doing nothing, yet."

Ok. Now, I've never been *here* before. Lisa quickly shifted focus to my left foot, squeezing and caressing with sensual lust. Then she grabbed my toes again and cracked the joints with pressure.

"Mmmm," I let out a faint moan. This seems to motivate her as she presses her fingers against the ball of my foot, easing out tension I didn't even know was there.

"Just relax, baby," she mumbled, as I felt her hard nipples brush my leg.

Before I knew it, Lisa took the belligerence to a new level. With aggressive boldness, she started kissing each one of my toes. And I'm not talking light pecks. She's French kissing each of my toes individually, with passionate attention.

"Fuuuuuuuuuck," I closed my eyes in disbelief. "Lisa...what...are....you....awww my gawd!"

I can't say that I've ever thought about getting my toes sucked – which is wild considering how much I love to suck toes when I'm in control. But this shit feels...oh my. What's the word I'm looking for? Amazing? No.

Sensational.

My toes being in Lisa's mouth feels fuckin' sensational. There's a sharp tingle running up my foot, going through my leg and up to my nut sack. It tickles, but then at the same time – it doesn't.

My dick gets harder. Lisa could feel it, too, cuz she started grinding her pussy and ass into it, moaning loudly. Her right hand finds its way to my right foot, as her mouth kept alternating between each of my left toes. She stops at my big toe and increases the suction. I can feel her drool running down to my heel, forming yet another puddle on the sheets.

My breathing gets heavier, faster. I'm lost in the moment now, grabbing the sheets with my fingertips. I can't explain how Lisa was able to force her way to control or how she got me to submit to this shit. But…I *like* it. I like it…almost too much.

What's crazier…is that Lisa worshipping my feet…has quieted and calmed the *beast* all the way down.

She moves over to my right foot now, switching back and forth from kissing to sucking…all while continuing to massage with slow force. The way her moans sound is giving me goosebumps. She's truly enjoying this shit, like it was an unknown, secret fetish for Big Booty Lisa. And I'm in total bliss, biting my lip to keep from squirming.

She sits up and stretches her legs out on top of mine, propping her ass into the bed space below my crotch for a quick second. I can't tell what she's doing now, but it feels like she's just staring at my feet, admiring her wet work. I sit up slightly, looking down at her bare back.

"Didn't I tell you to be still?" She turns her head to

the side without looking at me. "Scoot up...lay back down."

She gets up and reaches for the end table as I comply. My dick is throbbing with anticipation...which she notices as she puts the condom on for me...staring me in the eye, "You wanna fuck me again Rodney?"

"You know I do," I whispered.

"Yeah, I bet you do," she smirked at me. "That's what you been doing – fucking me over. I'm 'bout to fuck you now though. Keep ya hands to the side...don't move. And don't touch me."

"Come onnnn," I begged playfully.

"I'm not playing, Rodney," her voice was filled with sternness.

Lisa is still the only girl in the last few years I've allowed to call me by my government name, yet she knows the opportunity to ride me hardly ever comes around. She straddles me with arrogance, guiding it in slowly...pushing my chest in. My back is against the headboard...and she's on top of me, working her hips. This is all torture, but at least she ain't got my hands tied up. I wouldn't be able to take that.

She's lifting that ass up with each stroke and slamming down on my **wooD**...riding me with anger and frustration. Sweat beads are running down my face. I try to wipe them away, but she pushes my arm down. And I want to grab her ass..._sooooo_ bad...but she's not having it. She leans in towards my face, and I open my mouth to kiss her, but she's only repositioning herself, squatting on my dick now, bouncing up and down. She's biting her lip,

171

looking at me with a scowl.

The rush is exhilarating. I've had my way for long enough, Lisa is taking the upper hand back again. She's making me feel shame for being greedy...for fucking her sister out of belligerence and lust. I deserve this. Her pussy grips me...as she pauses momentarily before slamming down hard again. My dick jumps in her...she gasps with pleasure, "I told you not to move..."

My heart starts racing...as she starts bouncing up and down in a fury. Her ass seems so much more of a monster right now; my eyes start rolling. This is her moment of redemption...and she knows it. It's like she can read my mind.

I guess there's a reason Plan B is always only the backup plan. Sister A's sex is really the truth. She's screaming this with her eyes while she rides me...cutting them low at me.

Out of nowhere, grabbing my neck now. *Oh wow.* Her face close to mine...licking my lips. I lay still...muscles tight. She's cummin again. I can feel the warmth leaking onto my balls, drenching my thighs. It feels so relaxing. She keeps bouncing to her own femdom beat, "Cum with me, baby..."

This made my drool run down my jawline to my neck, "Hmmmm...."

I start humping now...and she doesn't stop me. I'm thrusting upward, meeting her stroke...it doesn't take long before it builds. This shit is turning me on something crazy...and she's in complete control. I never give up control like this...and yet I'm busting harder than ever before with Lisa. She slams down one last time and now she's grinding…clenching my dick and pulling all the nut out. She bites the side of my face as I stop moving.

"Damn, Lisa," I winced. "Ok, ok…"

"Don't go to sleep" she commanded. "You still on punishment. And don't touch me either."

"This what I get for being greedy, huh?" I panted, trying to catch my breath.

"*You* said it, not me, HoLLy," Lisa pointed out, rubbing it in verbally. "You know you a greedy ass nigga. So, come on…eat this pussy again."

I shake my head – but hey – fuck it. I dare not finish what I started…right???

Because 'greedy' is an understatement. I may never get enough of this shit. It's how it smells…that drives my cravings. It's how it feels…that guides my urges. And it's the *thrill* of it. The thrill of it still fuels the **monster** in my ~~beast~~, deep down within. And now lately…it fuels me just as much, if not more.

How did I ever even *think* I could get enough of this? As I stick my tongue back into Lisa's sweet honey, perhaps only the *cheat Gawds* really know the absolute truth. The truth is…I may never, *ever* get used to the *sweet* and *savory* taste of this shit. I'm addicted to it. I'm consumed by it. I'm forever a slave to the way that it controls me. The truth is…one day, this belligerent shit might be the death of me.

The belligerence is my biggest vice, my most potent, intangible drug. Even when I tried to erase the music from my life, the belligerence addiction remained strong. Even when I finally stopped fucking with Sug, my boldest thoughts somehow continued to flow freely.

Fucking Lisa's older sister was one of my most belligerent episodes to date. The idea of fucking *Sister B* in a ménage with my old bitch Carmen woulda been even more audacious. I've tried to keep Lisa at a distance over the years. And you would think that after fucking her sister…she woulda never gave me the pussy again. Yet here she is, fucking the shit outta me…this time, sucking toes and squirting on me with that juicy kryptonite Sug used to spray me with.

Is there a lesson to take away from all of this irony? I mean, I ain't talked to Sug in a couple of months, but maybe the Curse is using Lisa to tell me something about my former fountain of a toxic lover? Shit…I don't even care. Fuck Sug right now!!! With the way I'm getting drenched, I can't think clearly about either of my exes, even if I wanted to. The splashing soundwaves of this squirting pussy are too loud to devote real focus elsewhere.

The beast is right – this is a cold game I've grown to love playing. And I realize in this final moment of clarity that I'll likely never *truly* kick this habit. I realize now that I don't ever want to. I'm back on top of the world and Grandpa Jerry would be proud. I'm not making multiple baby mamas, but fucking siblings and living to tell the story is the ultimate source of empowerment for a cheater trying to bounce back. But living long enough to receive the opportunity to fuck *Sister A* again *after* the fact…well, that's as powerful as it gets.

Lisa is moaning at the top of her lungs now; her flower still relentlessly spraying my face. It almost feels like it's washing the stains away, for another fresh start.

174

"This shit 'a make for some damn good music if I ever get back in the studio," I think to myself silently. *"I'm hearing bars in my head again."*

"What is this? We getting back in the studio, nigga?!?"

"I don't know, nigga! Maybe!!! This belligerence shit be inspiring me, dawg."

Yeah, you outdone yourself this time, HoLLy. I can't even front," even my ~~beast~~ is surprised at how much he's rubbed off.

"I'm saying, be for real, bro! How many rap niggas you know that smashed sisters in real fucking life?"

Perhaps the takeaway lesson is – sometimes a little *HoLLy BeLLigerence* can go a long, unexpected way. Now I'm thinking, maybe I *should* keep fucking big sister Shonne, after all. I mean, what if she a squirter, too? What if *she* on some even more freakier shit now, too??? It's like they competing with each other at this point.

Better yet…nah. I wonder if **Sister C** follows me on *Twitter.*

Yeeeeaaaah…that might be the move. Maybe *Sister C* will help me *really* get used to this type of taboo sibling rivalry. It truly brings new meaning to the idea of a *family*

175

affair…right?

Maybe next episode…

FIN.
(Until We Cheat Again)

ABOUT THE AUTHOR

"*HoLLyRod*" – the author & creator of the highly controversial and raunchy storyline, *The Art of Cheating* – is the alter-ego and pseudonym for established writer Rodney L. Henderson Jr.

Since graduating with a Business Administration degree in Computer Information Systems from the *University of Central Missouri*, Henderson has showcased his writing skills in various forms of art – including radio commercials & music, as well as poetry & promo spots for fashion companies such as *DymeWear Inc* & *Ridikulus Kouture LLC*.

HoLLyRod's short story mini-series titled **The Art of Cheating Episodes** introduces readers to the many characters & mystery behind **HoLLyWorld** and *The Art of Cheating*, while chronicling the ups & downs of infidelity through experiences based on real life. The ongoing series has been re-released in a special Extended Author's Cut Edition.

AVAILABLE IN eBOOK & PAPERBACK FORMATS!!! AUDIO BOOKS COMING SOON!!!

Henderson currently resides in his home state of Missouri and spends most of his time managing & writing for *Angela Marie Publishing, LLC* – a company named after his late mother.

The Art of Cheating Episodes is published under *Lurodica Stories*, an erotica division of the publishing company.

"I just want to continue to be inspired at the notion of making her proud and keep my promise to share my talents with the world."

**www.HoLLyRods.com
www.facebook.com/TheArtOfCheating
www.twitter.com/TheCheatGods**

Next up on
The Art of Cheating…

SEASON 1 — EPISODE 4:
KeLLy's Revenge

You never think it could happen to you. When it comes to
The Art of Cheating, if you're gonna do ya dirt, the least you
can do is everything in your power to cover it up. HoLLy has
always known the rules, but this fourth flashback revisits
the night he was served up some of his own shit. After
receiving a tip call about KeLLy possibly creeping around,
HoLLyRod hits the highway, speeding home in a drunken
attempt to catch her in the act. With all the times he's
been unfaithful, he knows deep down that he probably
deserves it. But a broken heart is still a broken heart, even
the heart of a cheater…

EXTENDED AUTHOR'S CUT EDITION
AVAILABLE NOW

Also by HoLLyRod

The Art of Cheating Episodes
(Extended Author's Cut Edition)

SEASON 1
Episode 1 - Sassy
Episode 2 – Hangover
Episode 3 - HoLLy BeLLigerence
Episode 4 - KeLLy's Revenge
Episode 5 - The HooKup
Episode 6 – Ménages

SEASON 2
Episode 1 - Cyber Pimpin' **(12/22/22)**
Episode 2 - Campus Record **(2/15/23)**
Episode 3 – A Date with Karma **(4/20/23)**
Episode 4 – The Wedding Party **(6/19/23)**
Episode 5 – HoLLy & Sug **(8/23/23)**

SEASON 3
(Spring 2024)

Angela Marie Publishing
Presents

WDFFIL EP1: Facing the Music

The OFFICIAL Soundtrack to The Art of Cheating Episodes

AVAILABLE ON ALL MUSIC PLATFORMS

DOWNLOAD OR STREAM NOW!!!!

https://distrokid.com/hyperfollow/hollyrod/wdffil-ep1-facing-the-music-4